BOOKS BY CHRISTIE HARRIS

Confessions of a Toe-Hanger
Figleafing Through History (*With Moira Johnston*)
Forbidden Frontier
Let X Be Excitement
Mouse Woman and the Mischief-Makers
Mouse Woman and the Muddleheads
Mouse Woman and the Vanished Princesses
The Trouble with Princesses
Once Upon a Totem
Once More Upon a Totem
Raven's Cry
Secret in the Stlalakum Wild
Sky Man on the Totem Pole?
West with the White Chiefs
You Have to Draw the Line Somewhere
Mystery at the Edge of Two Worlds

The Trouble
with
Princesses

The Trouble with
Princesses

by

CHRISTIE HARRIS

DRAWINGS BY DOUGLAS TAIT

Atheneum · New York
1980

*To the Native People of the Northwest Coast,
who were the first to tell of these princesses*

LIBRARY OF CONGRESS CATALOGING IN PUBLICATION DATA

Harris, Christie.
The trouble with princesses.

SUMMARY: Retells stories about Northwest Coast princesses
and compares them with similar Old World princesses.
1. Tales. [1. Folklore. 2. Princesses—Fiction]
I. Tait, Douglas. II. Title.
PZ8.1.H227Tr   398.2'2   79-22129
ISBN 0-689-30744-6

Published simultaneously in Canada by
McClelland & Stewart, Ltd.
Manufactured by R. R. Donnelley & Sons,
Crawfordsville, Indiana
Designed by M. M. Ahern
First Edition

Contents

BEFORE YOU READ THE STORIES

Princesses were always important characters in the fairy tales of the Old World. Dressed in satins and sparkling with jewels, they ate sugarplums and walked in palace gardens or waited in castles for the Plumed Prince they would marry. They moved through magical worlds in golden coaches or on splendidly caparisoned horses. And often they faced dangers from witches or dragons or three-headed trolls.

There were princesses, too, in the "fairy tales" of the New World. And they were just as important.

On the Totem Pole Coast, the northern part of the Northwest Coast of America, princesses were extremely important, for they carried the royal bloodlines of the great families in the several clans. Only their sons could be the great chiefs. So they were carefully guarded in a world as filled with danger and magical happenings as was that of the Old World princesses.

Instead of satins and jewels, though, these princesses of the Far West wore luxurious fur robes and gleaming copper or glistening abalone-pearl ornaments. They lived in gigantic cedar houses splendidly carved and painted with clan emblems and family crests. They moved about in huge, high-prowed, totem-crested cedar canoes paddled by slaves.

Sharing a magnificent world of wild seas and rushing rivers, of forests and snow-peaked mountains, with animals and Spirit Beings, known as *narnauks*, these princesses were surrounded by the proud symbols of blood and rank.

Everyone in all the tribes belonged to one of the several great bloodlines; and this basic clan identity—Eagle, Raven, Bear, Wolf—was displayed on skin, house, canoe and other belongings. Each of these basic bloodlines branched off into great families, with family crests like Killer Whale, Rainbow, Frog, Sea Lion Head, Fireweed. . . . Then there were more personal emblems won by some valiant ancestor, emblems like One-Horned Mountain Goat. All these crests were proudly displayed on the totem poles that rose before the chiefs' houses.

With no books to record the history of the people and their emblems, the storyteller was all important. Especially at the magnificent potlatch feasts, the gifted storytellers would remind the people of their heritage. And many of the tales were more than exciting entertainment, more than a recounting of tribal history and a cherishing of ancient customs. Many were also a warning, an emotional reminder of what happened to a proud, wealthy people when it forgot to be worthy of its wealth and importance. When it failed to keep the sacred Laws of Life.

And when the potlatch drums throbbed in the enormous feast house and the firelight flickered on carved house posts and totem-painted screens, or on the regalia of the chiefs, when the people hushed themselves to hear a whispering, shouting, leaping, gesturing storyteller, they sometimes found themselves trembling or laughing with a "fairy tale" princess.

THE TROUBLE WITH PRINCESSES *was that, at times, they were spirited girls who had no intention of just staying there, doing nothing, when the situation was intolerable.*

In the European fairy tales, there was the King of Cornwall's daughter, who was most unwilling to stay tied to a rock until a prince rescued her from the dragon that was destined to eat her, especially since she knew herself to be much more skilled with the blade than was the prince who was destined to rescue her. She took matters into her own hands and rescued the prince.

Then there was Princess Rosette, who was shut up in a tower forever because it had been foretold that she would bring misfortune to her brothers. This spirited young lady decided to marry the mysterious King of the Peacocks. And though she did bring misfortune to her brothers, she also rescued them. And she married the King of the Peacocks.

And then there was the Icelandic Princess Hadvor. Her stepmother, who was really a witch, laid a spell on Prince Hermod; he had to live on a desert island as a lion by day and a man by night until Hadvor should burn the lion's skin. To accomplish this, the spirited young lady poured blazing pitch on a three-headed-giant, overcame his ghost, scaled a cliff and battled a whale-that-was-really-a-giant. In the end she rescued Prince Hermod and married him.

So it was, too, with the princesses of the Far West. Though there were no dragons or towers or peacocks in their world, there were as many fearful dangers. And as many spirited young ladies! The adventures of one of these is told in the story of "The Princess and Mountain Dweller."

1

The Princess and Mountain Dweller

It happened in the time of long ago, when things were different along the mountainous Northwest Coast. Then, wealth and social position were cherished. And the proper behavior of a marriageable princess was all important.

Now, as it happened, one proud and spirited princess—Maada—was none too happy with her sudden change from carefree girl to marriageable princess. She was like a deer deprived of its freedom. Now, instead of running joyfully along the beach and the trails, she was expected to move as a dignified young lady should, surrounded by a flutter of high-ranking attendants. Only her grandmother seemed to see her still as a child.

Her grandmother was keeper of a special box that held special food for special visitors. But she could never resist slipping bits of the special food to her two granddaughters, Maada and her little sister. And when she was challenged about the missing tidbits, she could never resist saying, "The old shaggy dog took it away from me." Though everyone knew where it had really gone.

One day she gave the two girls the very last bits of precious mountain sheep tallow. And that might not have mattered so much if a canoeload of important visitors had not arrived unexpectedly from somewhere along the river. And even that might not have mattered so much if the girls' father had not been head chief of the village, the natural host for such important visitors.

He was a man of great pride. His house was the biggest of the big, handsomely decorated cedar houses on the Street of Chiefs. His hospitality was famous. His small son was heir to a mighty chieftainship in another village. And his elder daughter was so beautiful that she was being sought in marriage by the noblest families along the coast. Indeed, the unexpected canoe carried one of the most desirable of these suitors.

When the big totem-crested canoe arrived, the chief sent his young men down to carry up the travellers' belongings. He put on a fine robe and ordered the Dance of Welcome. And he asked his wife to provide some special tallow tidbits so that the honored guests might chew the fat around the fire until a proper feast was prepared for them.

His wife went quickly to the grandmother, only

to be told that the last bit of precious tallow was gone. "The old shaggy dog took it away from me," the grandmother told her son's wife.

"Indeed?" the chief woman said, turning suspicious eyes on her two daughters. "Did you take the tallow?" she asked them in quiet anger.

Maada raised her head defiantly, while the little princess blinked back tears. They couldn't answer, for they had just snatched up the hard pieces of tallow from their wooden food dishes and popped them into their mouth to hide them, for their grandmother's sake, of course. They had also dropped mats over the telltale dishes.

Their mother glared at the uncomfortable girls. Then, after glancing furiously around, she snatched the mats off their food dishes. "There are hairs on these dishes," she said as she streaked an angry finger along the polished wood.

"The old shaggy dog's hairs," the grandmother suggested; and her eyes twinkled.

"Indeed?" the chief woman snapped. Then she grabbed Maada by the nose to make her open her mouth. She yanked out a piece of hard fat so fiercely that it scratched the inside of the girl's mouth.

"Glutton!" she stormed at her daughter. "A girl of your rank a glutton!" For gluttony was a terrible thing, especially for a princess. "You had better go off to the hills and marry Mountain Dweller, whose house is crammed with fine foods!" she raged. Then, turning away to share her husband's shame before the noble visitors, she looked for sweet hemlock sap cakes, which were much inferior to tallow as a special tidbit.

The princess was deeply shamed by the nose-grabbing and cheek-scratching, and by the taunt of "Glutton!" Yet she held her head high, as a princess must, and sat with the noble visitors until she could slip away to her sleeping place behind a screen at the rear of the great cedar house. As she slipped away, her eyes were flashing. And no sooner were she and her little sister safely behind the screen than she said, "I shall indeed go off to the hills and marry Mountain Dweller."

The little princess opened her eyes wide in dismay. For who knew what he would be like, this famous hunter whose house was crammed with fine foods. And people said there were terrible beings guarding the approach to his house. "But if you go, I'll go," she said. For the little princess adored her sister.

She helped dig a hole so that they could escape from under the rear wall. She helped place the long wooden food dishes in their sleeping places and cover them with fur robes. And then she crept with her angry sister into the dark woods. But who knew if the Wild Woman of the Woods and other fearsome narnauks might be watching? she thought, as she hugged her rich marten skin robe about her. For princesses, even escaping princesses, must wear rich marten skin robes.

Next morning, when the two girls did not appear, their mother went behind the screen to rouse them. "Get up and greet our guests!" she whispered fiercely to the two fur-covered mounds. She snatched off Maada's sleeping robe, only to be confronted with the long, handsomely decorated food dish. She snatched off the other robe. And there was the other dish. Then she saw the hole under the rear wall.

"The princesses have run away," she whispered to the relatives.

At once a group of hunters went off in search of them. And by skillfull tracking, they finally reached a spot near where the two girls were carefully hidden.

"Why don't we make a noise?" the little princess whispered. For she was most willing to be caught and taken back to her grandmother. "But . . . maybe not," she added as she caught the angry glint in her sister's eyes. Then they both almost held their breath until the searchers had gone off in another direction.

"Why don't we get caught?" Maada challenged as soon as she dared to raise her voice. "My nose is still bruised and my cheek is still hurting. I know what she said to me. And I know what she was thinking. That I'm a glutton, fit only to marry a chief whose house is crammed with fine foods." Giving her poor little sister no choice but to follow, she scrambled on up the mountain.

"I'm hungry," the little princess whimpered, as soon as she could catch her breath long enough to whimper.

"There'll be plenty to eat there," Maada grimly reminded her. Indeed, she too was hungry, having been too angry to eat with the noble visitors the night before. But she was *not* a glutton. She could go on forever without food, if need be.

They had gone a long, steep, hungry, weary way before they came upon a little mouse trying to get over a big log.

"Poor little mouse!" the little princess said, though she was much too weary to do anything but flop down where she was.

"Poor little mouse!" Maada agreed. And she lifted it gently over the big log.

In a minute they both heard a small, squeaky, but commanding voice call out, "Come in, my dears!" And when they glanced toward the voice, they were astonished to see a house there in the wilderness. A house decorated with Mouse totems.

"Mouse Woman?" the little princess gasped; and now her eyes were shining. For it was well known that the awesome little narnauk, who could appear to people as a mouse or as the tiniest of grandmothers, was a friend to young people who had fallen into trouble. "Mouse Woman!"

Indeed, when they entered the house, there was the tiniest grandmother they had ever seen, looking up at them with her big, busy mouse eyes.

"Why did you come here?" she asked them. But after one answering flash from Maada's eyes, she dismissed the question with a wave of a tiny hand. "You have helped me, my dear," she said, "so I shall help you." She placed some salmon by the fire to roast, and gave them a bowl of cranberries to be going on with. Then she waited until they had eaten well before she asked, "Why *did* you come here, Granddaughters?"

"Because, Grandmother," Maada answered, "because my mother said I should marry Mountain Dweller." There were tears to blink back, but not too many tears for her to notice that Mouse Woman's ravelly little fingers were itching to touch the long woolen tassels both princesses wore as ear ornaments. Being much too proud to expect something for nothing, she threw one of her ear ornaments into the fire—a proper way to offer a gift to a Spirit Being.

But the mouse in this Spirit Being was so strong that before the tassel was more than scorched, Mouse Woman spirited it out of the fire and her ravelly little fingers began tearing at it. Then, having received her favorite gift, she properly proceeded to give, in return, her favorite giving —advice to young people in trouble.

"I will direct you to Mountain Dweller's house," she told them. "But I warn you of the dangers you will face. Guarding the approach to the house are terrible beings disguised as everyday things."

"Terrible beings?" the little princess whispered, pulling her now-slightly-tattered marten skin robe tightly about her.

"Dangers, Grandmother?" Maada challenged. Clearly she was ready and willing to face even the Ogre. She had said that she would marry Mountain Dweller, and she would marry Mountain Dweller. "Tell me of the dangers, Grandmother!"

"I will tell you of three of the dangers," the tiny narnauk agreed. "And I will give you magical weapons to overcome them. But I cannot tell you of the fourth danger. That you must discover and deal with on your own."

"We will deal with it, Grandmother, when the time comes. But first, what of the other three dangers?"

Mouse Woman was gazing at Maada with interest. "Perhaps *you* are the one," she said, mysteriously. And while the little princess huddled fearfully into her marten skin robe, the big princess listened carefully to the tiny narnauk's advice about dealing with the fighting dogs, the floating kelp and Crushing-Mountain, which guarded the approach to Mountain Dweller's house. Then she thankfully placed Mouse Woman's gifts of a magical fish, a magical knife and a magical whetstone in the pouch at her waist, ready to be used against the three dangers.

"I don't really like fighting dogs and . . . and floating kelp and . . . crushing-mountains," the

little princess protested. Then, catching the flash in her sister's eyes, she added, "But maybe I'll like seeing them shrink back." Her voice was a small, frightened whisper.

In the morning, Maada took a purposeful breath and went boldly on her way, with her little sister following none-too-boldly behind her.

It all happened as Mouse Woman had said it would happen.

They had not gone far along the trail when two gigantic fighting dogs rushed at them, snarling and growling. Their long fangs were terrifying as the dogs crouched, ready to spring at the girls' throats; the growls in their fierce throats made the little princess cling fearfully to her trembling sister.

But even as she recoiled from the dogs in horror, Maada managed to throw the magical fish to them.

The fighting dogs pounced on it. And when they had devoured it, they began to gambol as playfully as mountain lambs, as Mouse Woman had said they would.

Nevertheless, she almost held her breath as she slipped past them, holding her little sister's hand tightly. Then, with a grateful prayer to the tiny narnauk, the two went on their way.

Soon they reached the water, as Mouse Woman had said they would. And there was the floating kelp, glittering in two separate rafts of writhing brown tubes and bobbing kelp heads. There was the canoe waiting for them. And there, at the foot of a tree near the canoe, was the moss.

With trembling fingers, Maada cut out a large clump of the moss with the magical knife, as Mouse Woman had instructed.

"Kelp in a *lake?*" the little princess whispered, swallowing.

"No doubt it's a bottomless lake with an underground channel going out to the sea," Maada said. A thought that did little to cheer her sister.

As they moved fearfully out onto the water, the two glittering rafts of writhing brown tubes and bobbing kelp heads began to move toward one another, from each side of the canoe. And as the girls paddled closer, great tubes rose from the water, flailing like the giant tentacles of Monster Octopus, threatening to encircle and crush the canoe.

Swallowing her alarm, Maada tossed the clump of moss between them. At once the floating kelp stopped writhing and flailing, and the two rafts moved back to let the canoe pass.

The canoe shot ahead, with the girls frantically paddling.

"I . . . don't like floating kelp," the little princess confessed as they beached the canoe on the far side of the mountain lake.

Right ahead of them rose Crushing-Mountain, with a great cut in its solid rock—the cut they must pass through to reach the house of Mountain Dweller. And even as they watched, the rock on each side of the cut began to close in, ready to crush them as soon as they had entered.

Even as she recoiled in horror, Maada hurled the magical whetstone into the cut.

At once the mountain shrank back on both sides of the cut, and the girls raced through without harm. But now there was no way to get back.

"I wonder what the fourth danger is," the little princess whispered, glancing fearfully about on all sides of the valley they had come into.

It was a beautiful alpine valley, dotted with small trees and brilliant with mountain flowers. And across the valley stood a big, handsome cedar house.

"At least there'll be lots of food there," the little princess said.

Then they saw the young man. Appearing from behind a clump of alpine fir trees, he was walking toward them.

"Maybe . . . he's the fourth danger," the little princess whispered. "Even a handsome young chief could be a danger." For sometimes dreadful beings appeared as young men to deceive you.

He was indeed a handsome young chief, with a hunting bow held close to his strongly muscled body. His headband, skin apron, and quiver were beautifully decorated with mountain symbols; and caribou ear ornaments swung as he walked.

"Welcome, Princesses!" he greeted them, after one glance of appraisal at their marten skin robes and their ornaments. "Why have you come here?"

"I have come to marry Mountain Dweller," Maada told him. And though her cheeks flushed, she held her head high.

The handsome young chief regarded her with interest. "Perhaps *you* are the one," he said, as mysteriously as Mouse Woman had said it. "I am Mountain Dweller. And I have been waiting for a proud and spirited princess." Without another word, he led them to his house across the valley.

They had known that Mountain Dweller was a famous hunter. Now they saw that he was also a wealthy one. For his house was even larger and finer than their father's. Its posts were magnificently carved; its screens were beautifully painted with mountain symbols. And on all sides great coppers glinted in the firelight. But they could see little of these treasures. For everywhere in the big windowless house were piles of handsomely decorated food boxes and bowls, and elegant wealth chests that were no doubt filled with precious fur robes and crested horn spoons and finely woven mats and carved food dishes.

Maada's eyes brightened over this crowded display of wealth as they had brightened over the handsome face and form of the man she had said she would marry. Yet. . . . She shivered in her fine marten skin robe as she pulled it more closely about her.

Mountain Dweller caught the slight movement.

Pointing to a large screen that cut off one corner of the great house, he said, "Do not go behind that screen, Princess! Do not even peep behind it! For there is danger."

"The fourth danger," the little princess mumbled, clinging to her sister's hand as she gazed at the screen with frightened eyes.

Maada swallowed as she nodded in agreement. This was indeed the fourth danger. And Mouse Woman had given her no magical weapon to hurl at it. Now, they were on their own.

They were indeed on their own. For after his visitors had eaten and slept and eaten again, Mountain Dweller picked up his bow and quiver. "Do not go behind that screen, Princess!" he warned. Then, with an anxious-yet-strangely-pleading look at the proud and spirited young lady, he went off hunting.

Sounds had begun to come from behind the screen.

"I think the fourth danger is an evil woman," the big princess whispered, picking up one of the sticks near the fire.

"But . . . we won't even peep, will we?" the little princess whispered back. She, too, picked up one of the sticks.

Her sister was sniffing the air. "An evil woman cooking," she went on. Whiffs of roasting meat and rendering fat had begun to waft over and around the screen. And with them came a terrifying odor of evil.

"We won't even peep, will we?" the little princess insisted, huddling behind one of the crowding chests.

"If we never know what the fourth danger is," her sister challenged, "how can we deal with it?"

"We could go home," the little girl suggested.

"How could we get back through CrushingMountain?" her sister challenged. "How could we stop the fighting dogs from attacking us?" She grasped her stick fiercely, but she knew it would be useless against terrible beings disguised as everyday things.

"Well . . ." the little girl said. But if she had any further suggestions, they were lost in quiet whimpers.

"I came here to marry Mountain Dweller," her sister reminded her. "So I shall marry Mountain Dweller." Yet there was fear as well as purpose in the dark eyes that kept glancing at the mysterious screen.

It was a long, lonely, terrifying day. Firmly clutching the stoutest sticks they could find, the girls walked in the lovely alpine meadow. But at last they had to go back into the crowded house, where sounds still came from behind the screen, and whiffs of roasting meat and rendering fat. And the terrifying odor of evil!

If only Mountain Dweller would not leave them on their own with the fourth danger! Yet it was late that evening before he came back from his hunting, and it was early the next morning when he went off. Again with the same warning, again with the same anxious-yet-strangely-pleading look at the proud and spirited young lady.

And so it went until the fourth day.

"Unless we want to stay cowering here forever," Maada said that morning, as soon as Mountain Dweller had gone off, "we must deal with the fourth danger." Fiercely grasping her stout stick, she moved stealthily through the piles of handsomely decorated food boxes and bowls and the elegant wealth chests, while her terrified little sister clung to her robe. Then, taking a deep breath and grasping her stout stick even more fiercely, she rounded the screen.

And there—almost touching her!—was the evil woman. Red-rimmed eyes leered at her from a wizened face and a straggle of dirty gray hair. One scrawny, claw-tipped hand clutched a side of mountain sheep standing on its end by the fire; the other held a dipper of flaming oil. And quick as the girl's gasp, the evil woman flung the burning oil over the side of meat and pushed the heavy flaming mass at the princess, to kill her.

But, also quick as a gasp, the princess bashed back with her stout stick, knocking the meat and the witch into the fire—where she went up in one quick, choking cloud of black smoke. And that was the end of the evil woman. Unless, as people later said, the choking cloud of black smoke turned into the choking clouds of black gnats that plagued hunters in the hills.

Maada sank to the floor, trembling with relief, while her little sister clung to her, howling.

Then Mountain Dweller was lifting her to her feet. "I knew *you* were the one," he said, embracing her with joy. "And you said you would marry Mountain Dweller."

First, though, he took them back to their father's house, with a gift of fine foods. And now Crushing-Mountain did not try to crush them; the floating kelp did not try to encircle and crush their canoe; the fighting dogs stayed as quiet as mountain lambs. For the evil was gone from the hills. Unless, as people later said, the gnats that pestered them were the evil woman. But that was a danger that even the little princess could deal with.

When they neared the village, they heard sounds of mourning. And when they met the young brother, who was heir to a mighty chieftainship in another village, they saw that his face was blackened in mourning for them.

He stared at them in alarm, then turned to race, shrieking, back to the village.

"He thinks we're ghosts," Maada told Mountain Dweller.

"My sisters! My sisters!" the small prince shrieked as he rushed into the village.

"You're sure it's your sisters?" his mother demanded, grasping his heaving shoulders in desperate hope. Her tear-stained face, too, was blackened in mourning for her daughters.

In answer, the boy raced back to his sisters.

Fearfully snatching a tatter from his younger sister's robe, he turned to race off again.

"It *is* the princesses!" everyone cried out, looking at the tatter. For only princesses wore fine marten skin robes. And they all rushed out to welcome the lost girls and the handsome young chief who came with them.

The proud and spirited princess married Mountain Dweller, as she had said she would. Then, with slaves to serve her, she went back to the magnificent-but-crowded house by the alpine meadow. And it was much less crowded when her husband had sent many well-filled food boxes and bowls to her family as a marriage gift.

Indeed, Mountain Dweller continued to send so many gifts of fine foods, and there was always so much precious mountain sheep tallow in the special box, that the grandmother never again had to say, "The old shaggy dog took it away from me."

❧ ❧ ❧

THE TROUBLE WITH PRINCESSES was that often their parents could find no one they thought worthy of their precious daughter. Pressed to let her marry, sometimes they arranged for the eager suitors to accomplish almost impossible tasks.

In the Old World fairy tales there was, for instance, the king who set his daughter on top of the glass hill with three golden apples in her lap. Only the man who could ride up the slippery slope and get the golden apples could have her for his wife. There was also the sultan who promised the Arabian princess's hand to the one who could find the most extraordinary rarity. And there was the king who made his daughter the prize for the one who should build a ship that would float on both land and sea. The trouble with these contests was that usually the unsuccessful suitors were to lose their heads.

Although it was sometimes a kind heart that helped the lucky suitor win the princess, more often it was sharp wits. When Princess Diamantina was the prize for the one who could find her suffering father's healing slipper, a young apothecary who used his wits to produce a healing ointment finally won her. It was Puss in Boots's wiliness that won a princess for his master. And it was certainly sharp wits rather than a kind heart *or even valor that won a princess for the Brave Little Tailor who had "killed seven at a blow." Seven flies!*

And so it was at times with the marriageable princesses of the Far West. With one of these, though, it was not a doting parent who arranged the contest, but an angry aunt who was something of a witch. True to fairy tale tradition, however, it was the suitor who used his wits who won the princess in the story of "Elk Maiden."

2

Elk Maiden

IT WAS IN THE TIME of very, very long ago, a time
when not all of Earth's creatures had yet taken on
their final form.

At this time, there were animals who were truly
animals, and people who were truly people. But
there were also the Myth People. They looked and
acted like human beings except when they put on
their other form and seemed to be ravens or sea
gulls or wolves or mountain goats.

Now among these Myth People were Elk Man
and Elk Woman, a chief and his wife, who had one
child, a daughter known as Elk Maiden. Because
they lived inland, in a remote area, there were few
young men to see how beautiful Elk Maiden was.
And of the few there were, none seemed suitable
for so lovely a princess.

She, finding life lonely in the remote area,
longed for a young man who would carry her off
to a well-peopled village. And as time went by and

still no suitable youth appeared, she began to be most unhappy.

"We must do something to find her a husband," Elk Woman said.

"Or if *we* can't, perhaps we could send her off to her aunt at the coast," Elk Man suggested.

"*That* aunt?" the mother protested. For that aunt was something of a witch.

"At least there's no shortage of young men in her village," the father pointed out.

Indeed there was no shortage. For that aunt was chieftainess of the strange Village of Young Men. That aunt had gathered together an assortment of youths from among the different tribes of Myth People. The only things the young men had in common were their youth and their dedication to hunting skills. Each had chosen to leave his own village to become a superb hunter.

"Well . . ." Elk Woman said, brightening considerably as she thought about the Village of Young Men. "We must do something to find her a husband."

So it was agreed that Elk Maiden should set out for her aunt's village. And since there was really no one suitable to send with her, she would travel alone. A young lady as fleet-footed and wary as she would be safe in the wilderness.

No word was sent ahead to the chieftainess, in case she might object.

Indeed, none was needed, for the aunt was truly

something of a witch. No sooner had Elk Maiden started out on her travels than the old woman began to watch her in spirit journeys.

"Trouble!" she croaked, waking from her first dream journey in a rage. A beautiful girl would be nothing but trouble in the Village of Young Men. Completely forgetting that they had left their own villages because nothing helped a hunter's luck more than staying clear of love, the young men would all want to marry her. They would begin to quarrel over her. And the chieftainess's firm rule would be shattered.

But not if she could help it! she thought, narrowing her snapping eyes and grinding her yellowed old teeth. If only she could pounce on the girl as a mountain lion! she thought. Or butt her down a steep mountain as a sharp-horned goat! But she could do nothing to stop the princess. The ties of blood were stronger than a witch's power, for the ties of blood were sacred.

Day after day and night after night, watching Elk Maiden's approach, the chieftainess put her wits to work. The girl would have to come. But then she must be dealt with. And the young men must be dealt with.

When Elk Maiden was but a few days' journey from the village, her aunt craftily put into motion a plan to deal with all the young people.

First she sent for Night Hawk, a youth with a strong voice. "Go through the village!" she commanded. "Cry out that my beautiful niece is coming to visit me! And if any young man wishes to win her for his wife, let him come to my house at sunset!"

Night Hawk ran through the village, crying out the astonishing news. A beautiful maiden was coming! Someone could win her for his wife!

By sunset, every young hunter in the village had questioned the belief that a hunter's luck depended on keeping away from women; every last one had decided that—even if it did!—*he* wanted to marry Elk Maiden.

At sunset, every youth in the Village of Young Men arrived at his chieftainess's big carved-cedar house. And the house throbbed with excitement.

Night Hawk pounded the floor four times with the carved Talking Stick. Then the chieftainess spoke. "Young men!" she called out as her snapping eyes glanced over the eager faces. "My niece is coming to visit me. And Elk Maiden is so beautiful that you will all want to marry her. So I have looked at each of you and thought of all of you. Yet I can find no one of you more worthy than the rest of you. So I have decided to give all of you an equal chance to win the princess. You will race for her. She will be placed at one end of the village, you at the other. And whoever first catches her shall have her for his wife."

"Very fair!" called out Deer, who knew himself as the most fleet-footed. "An equal chance for all!"

"Equal? What chance have I in a race to catch Elk Maiden?" protested Tortoise, who, although a most worthy youth, was by no means fleet of foot.

"What chance has a slow fellow like you to be a suitable husband for a fleet Elk maiden?" countered Wolf, who, like Deer, was sure that *he* would catch the princess.

Shouts and counter-shouts rose on all sides.

Four thumps of the carved Talking Stick stopped the hubbub.

"Young men!" the chieftainess called out. "It will be fair to all of you, for I shall give the slow runners a head start."

Then the arguments started over how much of a head start was fair for this one or that one. Even before Elk Maiden arrived, she had shattered the peace of the famous village.

"When?" rose the clamor. "When will she arrive?"

Four thumps of the Talking Stick again restored order.

"Only I will know when she is to arrive," the chieftainess told them. "And I forbid any of you to leave the village until she does so."

Accustomed to discipline, the young hunters stayed in the village. Indeed, it was the only way to keep an eye on the chieftainess, who, sooner or later, would be slipping off to meet her niece. Also, it was the best way to keep an eye on one another, to see that none gained an unfair advantage. And by staying in the village, the youths could properly attend to their face paint and hair feathers and other marks of manly appearance.

Secretive as she was, and stealthy as she tried to be, the chieftainess was seen by every eye in the village as she slipped off into the forest one day.

In the meantime, Elk Maiden was nervously coming closer. Would her aunt be surprised to see her? she wondered. Would she be angry? And all those young men! Her previous eagerness gave way to dismay as she neared the village.

She was moving slowly when she glimpsed her aunt coming to meet her. And at sight of the craggy figure with black eyes snapping in a craggy face, Elk Maiden swallowed.

"Niece, you are welcome!" the chieftainess greeted her. And her long yellowed teeth showed in a smile that did nothing to lessen the girl's nervousness. "Follow me to the village!"

They walked silently along the trail. Then they rounded a large rock outcropping. And there was the village, with its houses and crestpoles bright along the curving beach. There were the young men, lining the path to her aunt's house.

Never had Elk Maiden seen so many young hunters! All watching her! Her cheeks flamed with embarrassment. Her head drooped to fix her gaze modestly on the ground. So many young men! All watching her! Thankfully she darted in through

the opening in her aunt's carved portal pole.

Now the hubbub from outside was like the humming of bees and the crying of sea gulls and the yipping of coyotes. Elk Maiden knew a moment of longing for the peace and quiet of her inland home.

"If the peace of my village is not to be completely shattered," her aunt said, "if my young men are not to start harming one another, we must have the race tomorrow."

"Race?" Elk Maiden asked her.

"Whoever catches you first will marry you."

Elk Maiden opened her mouth, then swallowed her protest. Eager as she had been to have a husband, she was dismayed by this scramble. She would have liked time to look over the suitors and choose one who caught her fancy.

"Your finest clothes!" the chieftainess commanded when dawn brought the greening of a new day. And soon Elk Maiden stood before her in a pale doeskin dress elegantly decorated with painted symbols and dyed moose hair embroidery. Feathers and dyed woolen tassels were in her dark hair. Discs of glistening blue-green abalone mother-of-pearl hung from her ears. And the excitement of the occasion made her cheeks bloom like wild roses.

When she was led out into the morning, a murmur of admiration rose from all sides. And every eye followed her as her aunt led her to the far end of the village, to where a trail led away toward a snow-peaked mountain.

Who would catch this most beautiful of maidens?

"Who will catch me?" Elk Maiden wailed to her aunt.

"No one," the Chieftainess answered. "For I will invoke *powers*. I will do what I will do while you circle back behind the village and slip into my house."

Elk Maiden opened her mouth to speak again, then closed it to swallow. *Circle back behind the village and slip into my house?* How could she do that with all the young men's eyes on her? And WHY would she do it? Her confusion grew with her dismay as she waited for her aunt to arrange the young men at the other end of the village, near the large rock outcropping. But she did glance warily about to see which way she must go to reach her aunt's house.

Now, as it happened, eyes sharper than Elk Maiden's were watching her aunt. Lynx, a handsome, quick-witted youth, had entered the race like all the others. Somewhat crafty himself, he was always alert for craftiness in others. So, while the other young men had eyes only for the princess and for their own places at the start, Lynx was watching the chieftainess. He noticed that while she was placing the protesting youths in their proper places, she was quietly shaking a medicine rattle. She was up to something, he decided.

Then there was silence, the tense silence of waiting.

Hearts thumped. Who would win this most beautiful of maidens?

"Elk Maiden . . . young men!" the Chieftainess called out, still shaking her medicine rattle, but now also looking upward as she combed the air with the white eagle tail she held in her other hand.

She *was* up to something. Lynx was certain. She was invoking some *Power*. Some *Sky Power?* She intended to trick the racers. Well! He intended to trick her!

"Elk Maiden! . . . young men!" she called out again. "Ready? . . . RACE!"

Scores of feet thudded. INTO SUDDEN BLACKNESS! For, at the moment of the signal, black clouds raced across the sky. In an instant, it seemed, day was as dark as night. And caught in the confusion of sudden blackness, the racers ran into one another.

Elk Maiden, as stunned as the racers, groped her way toward the back of the houses.

Lynx abandoned the race. He peered through the blackness for some sign of the chieftainess. There! He was sure he had glimpsed her darting toward the back of the houses.

Now the racers were not only running into one another; they were bumping into crestpoles and trees.

Groping his way along the fronts of the houses, Lynx kept peering into the open spaces between them.

Soon the racers began to grab one another, crying out, "I have her! I have her!" Only to be pushed off by an indignant rival.

"She's mine!" Wolf shouted as he clutched a strip of loose bark hanging from a cedar tree. Thinking it was Elk Maiden, he threw out his arms to embrace her. And found branches in them.

"She's mine!" Deer protested, grabbing Wolf's hair.

Elk Maiden gasped as she felt someone grab her. WHO . . . ? In an instant she knew it was her aunt, dragging her along with fierce, scrawny fingers.

Lynx kept peering into the open spaces between the houses. There! That was the chieftainess dragging someone. SHE had caught the princess!

"Quick!" the chieftainess said, almost throwing her niece in through the opening in her carved house pole. And the firelight showed a red glitter in the witch eyes. "Quick!" she said again. "Hide in the basket!" It was a big new basket she had woven while waiting for the girl's arrival. And it rested high on a platform with several wealth chests, close to the roof in a shadowed corner. "Quick! Into the basket!"

Too stunned to do anything but obey, Elk Maiden climbed swiftly up to the platform and hid herself in the basket, while her aunt shook her medicine rattle and combed the air with her white eagle tail.

Outside, as suddenly as it had come, the darkness vanished. The sun shone again on a bedlam of confusion.

"Where is she?" disheveled youths clamored. "Who has caught her?"

Then there was silence. Clearly, no one had caught her.

"The SUN!" someone cried out. And a stunned silence marked the realization that the Sun himself had wanted so beautiful a maiden. It was why he had left the sky, causing the sudden blackness. Battered youths sank to the ground in dismay. The Sun himself had come out of the sky to snatch the prize for himself. For what else could account for the startling darkening of the world in the morning?

The crestfallen young men straggled into their chieftainess's house to report their defeat.

"The Sun himself has taken the prize," Deer told her.

It was what they all thought.

All except one!

Lynx's sharp eyes were the only ones searching among the boxes and baskets for some sign of Elk Maiden. And he noticed the new basket, high on a platform with several wealth chests, close to the roof in a shadowed corner. That was where the chieftainess had hidden the vanished maiden?

For days and days, while the others settled sadly back into their old ways, Lynx found reason after reason to visit the chieftainess. Once he took her a specially fine salmon. Then a basket of roots. And then a haunch of deer meat. But enter as often and as suddenly as he would, he saw no sign of the vanished maiden. Perhaps the Sun had indeed left the sky to snatch the prize for himself. Yet . . . that basket! It was clearly a new basket, and unusually large for a cradle-shaped basket. Somehow, he had to see what was in that basket.

Easier decided than done, however. For, night or day, the chieftainess never seemed to stir from her house.

Neither did Elk Maiden. Hidden in the basket, high under the roof in the dark corner, never going out into the beautiful sunshine, never feeling the invigorating breezes, she was far more unhappy than she had ever been in her old home.

"I can't stay here!" she protested again and again.

"You can't go out," her relentless aunt countered. "Not until the young men are certain that the Sun has indeed taken you. Then, some night, I will slip you out of the village, and you can start back to your own home."

But the night was long in coming. Almost suffocating under the roof, Elk Maiden began to poke with her little woman's knife at a crack between two roof planks above her. What were a few drops of rain if she could catch a glimpse of the sky?

Too, her ears began to notice that a certain young man often came to the house with gifts of food for the chieftainess. And once when he was there, she waved a hand above the basket in the hope that he might see it—though she also hoped that her fierce aunt might not see it.

Lynx did see it, though his eyes betrayed nothing to the witch he was facing. So Elk Maiden *was* up there in the basket! His eyes narrowed over a plan that had been growing in his mind. Because of a strange dream, he knew how to free the Princess, win her for himself, and wreak vengeance on the trickster.

One night, after the entire village had apparently accepted the fact that the beautiful maiden had vanished from the Earth, Lynx crept stealthily toward a certain corner of the chieftainess's roof. He moved silently on the planks until he knew he was directly over the basket. Then, as he was considering how best to make a small hole, he spotted the widening of the crack done by the Princess's knife. He peered in. And there was Elk Maiden, asleep in the big cradle-shaped basket.

"Aha!" he crowed in silent triumph, though he had known that she was there. And his eyes glinted with mischief as he began to put his dream-given plan into action. The chieftainess would soon see that she was not the only one who could trick the village.

Closing his eyes to invoke the mighty Spirit that

had sent him the dream, he gathered moisture in his mouth. Then he carefully aimed a drop of spittle at Elk Maiden's soft skin. And slipped away as silently as he had come.

For four nights he did this, since it was well known that the supernatural must be called upon four times. Four times he invoked the Spirit that had sent him his dream-plan. Four times he aimed a drop of spittle at Elk Maiden's soft skin. Four times he slipped away as silently as he had come. Then he went back to his hunting and hunting rituals as whole-heartedly as if Elk Maiden had never existed. But always he waited for what he knew was to happen.

Because this was a supernatural happening among the Myth People, it happened astonishingly fast. Within days, Elk Maiden was aware of a swelling within her. Within several more days, her aunt's witch eyes were glaring at her. For clearly the princess was about to have a child.

"Who has been with you?" the chieftainess screamed at Elk Maiden.

"No one has been with me," the princess tearfully assured her aunt. Disgrace had come to her, but she was innocent, as the other well knew.

"Someone has played a trick on us," the chieftainess agreed, furious to think that anyone *could* play a trick on her. "Well! We shall soon find out WHO." The snapping of her black eyes foretold trouble for the trickster.

Yet watch as she would, and dream as she would, she had not discovered the WHO by the time a baby was born to the princess. Clearly a Spirit child, he had come in an astonishingly brief time. And he grew by leaps and bounds, unlike a real child.

Then the chieftainess had a dream that really set her eyes snapping. "The time has come to find out WHO has brought disgrace to the village," she told Elk Maiden. "Hide yourself and the child in the basket until I call you!"

She sent for Night Hawk. "Go through the village!" she commanded. "Say that I have found my niece, and that she has been delivered of a child. At sunset tomorrow, every young man in the village will come to my house with a gift for the child!"

Her dream had told her that the child would reject the gift of anyone except his father.

As soon as he had recovered from his own surprise at the news, Night Hawk went out to tell the others. And once more it was like the humming of bees and the crying of sea gulls and the yipping of coyotes as every young hunter discussed the astonishing news. Was this the Sun's child? Coming so soon after Elk Maiden's disappearance! Would she and her child come to Earth on a sunbeam? And what should the young men present as gifts to a child who was so clearly supernatural? Knowing that the great Sun himself would see their gifts,

WHAT should they offer?

All were as busy as beavers until the time came. Then, one after another, the young men came into their chieftainess's house. They gazed in amazement at Elk Maiden and her child, for no one had seen them arriving. Each offered his gift: an unusual feather, a tinkle of seashells on a leather thong, a tiny paddle, a bag of eagle down, a carved figure. . . . Yet, however beautiful the gift was, the child pushed it away from him—while the chieftainess watched with her black eyes glittering.

At last every hunter had offered his gift. And every gift had been rejected.

"Someone is missing," the chieftainess said.

"Lynx!" several youths cried out, after glancing about.

"Night Hawk!" the Chieftainess commanded. "Summon Lynx!" And the youth went out swiftly, calling in his strong voice for the missing young man.

In minutes he returned with Lynx. The child crowed and reached out his hands for the polished wooden ball the handsome young man carried. And at once he began to play with it.

There was a gasp of astonishment. Then utter silence.

The chieftainess broke the silence. "In a dream, I saw that the child would accept only the gift of his father." And when the amazement that greeted these words had been silenced by four thumps of the Talking Stick, she went on, "What shall be done to the young man who has brought disgrace to our village? Death is too good for him!"

"Death is too good for him!" a score of angry voices echoed. And all the young men glared at the offender.

"He shall marry the disgraced one," the chieftainess continued. "But he shall possess her in loneliness and starvation. I have long been thinking of moving across the inlet to my other village, where I have heard the hunting is better. We will move at once, leaving Lynx and his family to survive as best they can in a place where the offended Spirits will send no more fish, no more game, no more favors."

"Just punishment!" the young men agreed.

"Then prepare to move tomorrow!"

Though they rushed to obey, each took time to circle round by Lynx and give him a hard kick or an angry blow. By the time they were gone, he was too battered and bruised to stand upright.

Elk Maiden, who had watched the whole scene in shame and embarrassment, now came forward. And though she lashed Lynx with her tongue, she also attended to his injuries. At least he had managed to get her out of that terrible basket. For that she was grateful. Too, he *was* a handsome youth, and no doubt kinder than her aunt. She went willingly with him to his house.

Next day, as the angry young men were about

to leave with their chieftainess, many of them felt a surge of compassion for the beautiful princess. It was hard for a young woman and her child to be doomed to starvation. For, caught in the wrath of the witch, the couple would find fish and game vanished from around the village they had dishonored. Moving secretively—especially when Raven, the only gluttonous youth in the village, was around—many left food for Elk Maiden to find in their houses. Then, at their chieftainess's command, they paddled away across the inlet.

Touched by the compassionate glances some of the young men had turned on her, Elk Maiden went into their houses. And her heart warmed to their kindness, for her aunt had left no food. Finding the food the youths had left, she carefully noted *which* houses. If the chance ever came, she would be kind to those who had been kind.

Refusing to think of the doom her aunt had foretold, she talked cheerfully of the hunting her husband would do as soon as he was once more able.

And he, for his part, prepared as cheerfully to do it. But the night before he was to leave, he had a strange dream. "My Guardian Spirit came to me in my dream," he told Elk Maiden. "He told me I was destined to become a great chief. Then he showed me the pattern of a strange bow and arrow, saying that with such a weapon, I would always find game at the back of the village."

So, instead of starting off as he had planned, he took precious time to fashion a bow and arrow after the pattern he had seen in his dream. And no sooner had he left the village than fat deer sprang out on all sides.

"The Spirits are not offended," Elk Maiden pointed out. And things became happy in the deserted village. In fact, there was so much food that Elk Maiden gave her small son a ball of precious mountain goat tallow to chew at. And the child crowed with delight.

🌸 🌸 🌸

ACROSS THE WATER, things were sadly otherwise. No sooner had the young men settled into their new home than they found that the plentiful game had mysteriously vanished. The best hunters could find nothing in the longest day's search. Soon famine threatened the village. And angry glances began to turn on the chieftainess, whose power was clearly leaving her.

Perhaps she was the one who had offended the Spirits, they muttered to one another. After all, the youths had begun to realize, before Lynx had played a trick on anybody, she had played a trick on everybody. She had tricked all of them out of a fair chance to win the most beautiful of maidens.

Day by day the angry mutterings increased. Famine could come to them. To them—the dedicated youths who had forsaken their proper homes and families to win the great hunting power the chieftainess had promised! For them to go back to their families—starving!—was a shame not to be borne by proud young hunters.

Now, as it happened, no one in the new village dreaded famine more than Raven, the one and only glutton among the young men. And one day, with hunger gnawing at him, he put on his magical flying blanket to fly as a raven. And though even the thought of flight was exhausting to one so near starvation, he went back across the inlet. For he suspected that some of the young men had left food in their houses, and Elk Maiden might not have found it. Too, a hunter as sharp-eyed as Lynx might have found something; and a friend as crafty as Raven could find a way to get some of the something.

He lighted thankfully on a roof in the deserted village. And almost at once his sharp eyes found Elk Maiden's chubby child playing with a ball—a ball of MOUNTAIN GOAT TALLOW! Without a second thought, he flew down, pounced on the ball and tried to swallow it whole. But it stuck in his raven throat.

The howl of the outraged child brought his mother running. Outraged in turn, she seized the bird by its neck and forced it to disgorge her child's ball. Then she gave the robber a good shaking. "How could you rob my child?" she angrily demanded.

To her amazement, the bird shed its magical

flying blanket. And there stood a youth—a youth whose bones almost rattled in his loose skin.

"How did this happen?" the shocked princess asked. For she recognized him as one of the young hunters who had left the village. Then her eyes narrowed with suspicion. Having suffered from her aunt's trickery before, she was alert for more trickery.

"Everything goes wrong across the inlet," Raven wailed, still keeping his greedy gaze on the precious goat fat. "Only pride keeps the starving young men from returning to their old homes."

"So!" Elk Maiden said. "Your chieftainess has fallen into the plight she wished on me." Still bitter over her aunt's desertion of herself and her child, when she had known that both were blameless, she added, "Go back and tell her I rejoice in her misfortune!" Yet, glancing again at the youth's gaunt face, she had not the heart to dismiss him so cruelly. "Eat all you wish," she said, relenting. "And come every day to eat, if you wish. But do not tell the others!" For if the witch learned of their good fortune, who knew what she might do?

As long as it ensured food for his greedy gullet, Raven would promise anything—especially anything that kept him from sharing it with others.

And so it was that every day he put on his magical flying blanket, flew across the inlet, gorged himself, and returned back across the water, growing fatter by the day.

And the starving young men—angry at first with Lynx for his trickery, then increasingly angry with their chieftainess, who had started the trickery in the first place—now began to be furious about Raven. Clearly he had found a source of food. And just as clearly—glutton that he was!—he was keeping all the food to himself, an unthinkable crime in the Far West.

So one day the others seized him and threatened to kill him if he didn't tell them where he had found food. And he, realizing that food wouldn't be much good to him after he was dead, told them. "Across the inlet in our old village, Lynx, Elk Maiden and their child are living in plenty. They give me food every day, but made me promise not to tell you."

So! The game had NOT vanished! Now the anger turned away from Raven, back to the chieftainess, who should have known how things would be. "We are moving back across the water tomorrow," they told her.

Helpless in face of this sudden united resolve of strong-minded young men dedicated to hunting power, the chieftainess turned wily. "Young men!" she called out, with vinegary sweetness. "I was about to make that announcement myself." There would be ways to get back her power over them, she felt sure. And to get rid of Elk Maiden, who had started all the trouble in the first place.

※ ※ ※

FAR ACROSS THE WATER, Elk Maiden saw them coming. And though her eyes glinted with continuing anger against her cruel aunt, she remembered the food many of the young hunters had left for her in their houses. She remembered which houses. And with her husband's help, she swiftly carried food to those houses—as much as she had found, and a bit more. She put no food in her aunt's house.

The little family did not go down to the beach to welcome the returning chieftainess and her young men. The youths, faint with hunger and exhausted by paddling, staggered to their own houses. Those who found Elk Maiden's food fell on it like ravening wolves. Those who found no food staggered on to Lynx's house to pick up the scraps the Princess had thrown out for that purpose.

For several days the couple stayed in their house, though each day they threw out a basketful of scraps, which starving young hunters fell on like scavenging sea gulls. And the glances they turned on their chieftainess grew more and more angry. This is what she had brought them to. Scavenging for scraps!

Then, when Elk Maiden thought the time was right, she asked her husband to invite the village to the great feast she had been preparing. And when the young men had come and had feasted and feasted, Lynx told them of his dream and of his Guardian Spirit's promise that he should become a great chief.

"He was meant to be our chief," young hunters

murmured to one another. For this had never been a traditional village with proper hereditary chiefs. It was clear, now, who had had the right of it and the wrong of it in what had happened in the village. It was clear, now, whom the Spirits favored.

Right then and there it was decided that Lynx should be Chief of the Village of Young Men.

With little delay, he was ceremonially seated on a chief's seat at the rear of the fire, with Elk Maiden beside him and her child in her arms. And since Lynx had found supreme hunting power with a wife, clearly there were other changes to be made in the Village of Young Men. Though all agreed that staying away from women was a necessary part of any hunting ritual, they also agreed that there was a limit to all things.

In all the excitement, few noticed the deposed chieftainess slip away with her black eyes snapping. And as far as anyone could ever find out, she was the one who *did* vanish from the Earth. But no one suspected that the Sun himself had snatched *her* up as a prize.

✿ ✿ ✿

THE TROUBLE WITH PRINCESSES was that
sometimes they fell into dire straits.

In the Old World fairy tales, there was the
princess who, on her way to her wedding, was
betrayed by her maid. She found herself serving
as the poor Goose Girl. Then there was the
princess who became Master-Maid to a giant. And
then there was Kari Woodengown, whose wicked
stepmother starved her and beat her and set her to
work in the fields. After running away with a
magical blue bull, she lived in a pigsty, wore a
wooden gown and served in a strange castle until
a prince and a golden shoe saved her.

So it was, too, with the princesses of the Far
West. Sometimes they fell into dire straits, and it
took magic to rescue them.

One of these was Princess Djoon, who fell into
dire straits indeed. And it was all on account of
witchcraft—witchcraft brought on by what the
people had done. She was remembered in the old
feasthouses as the one who brought an
understanding of magic and witchcraft to a very
confused people.

What happened to her, and what she did about
it, is told in the story "Witchcraft."

3

Witchcraft

IT WAS IN THE TIME of very long ago, when people did not yet fully understand about magic and witchcraft.

The princess who was sadly caught up in witchcraft was of the Raven Clan, like her mother, and not of the Eagle Clan like her father. For this was the way of the northern people of the West Coast.

Now Princess Djoon had grown up with slaves to cater to her every whim. But her great Raven Family had been mysteriously wiped out. Only she and two young Raven commoners—two girls—had survived; only the carved posts of mighty Raven House were left standing. So, with no place to live, no family to care for her, no relatives to arrange a marriage for her, and no slaves to serve her, she wandered about alone and unkempt, scavenging like a sea gull.

Only an aunt, her father's sister—an Eagle like him—did what she could for the poor orphaned

princess. But there was little she could do. For the
Eagles, too, were in sore straits. Indeed, it seemed
that the whole village was caught up in evil witchcraft. And since no one really understood about
magic and witchcraft, no one knew what to do.
Everyone was terrified of doing anything that
might bring on more bad luck.

There was so little they could be sure of! But
clearly there *was* magical power in animals. So the
hunters continued to hang bear claws around their
necks to capture some of that power for themselves. They continued to put eagle feathers in their
hair to make themselves stronger, swifter and more
keen-sighted. But all in vain, it seemed. Still, chiefs
kept on wrapping themselves hopefully in the skin
of seat otters or in the wool of mountain sheep so
that it could lend them the power and the warmth
of the animal it was part of. Women put on shredded cedar bark garments to get the protection of
the spirits of the mighty cedars.

But the Ravens had worn skins, claws and
feathers, they reminded one another. Indeed, for
some time before the tragedy, the mighty Ravens
had even decorated their heads with golden tufts
of feathers from the wild canaries that brightened
their world; Raven boys had vied with one another
to catch them with swift cord-and-stones. They had
done it to enhance the brightness of their own
Spirit selves. Yet the terrible sickness had come to
them. And the wild canaries had left the woods
around the village. Although the birds had gath-

ered enough hairs to line a multitude of nests, they had vanished as mysteriously as the game animals that had vanished later. And now, facing starvation, people were terrified of doing anything that might make matters worse.

So it was that when some of the women were setting off one day to dig roots and Djoon begged to go with them, the women muttered fearfully to one another. "We must not take her," they said. "A girl as dirty and unlucky as that will only bring us bad luck."

Desperate to go, Djoon caught the gunwale of a canoe and tried to climb in. But the fearful women struck her fingers with their paddles.

"We can't leave her to starve," the aunt told her children. And though they were as fearful as the others, they did take the ragged, orphaned princess along. They let her camp with them in their brush hut on the root-digging island.

But when they were ready to leave for home, the princess was missing.

"What's the matter with her?" anxious, guilt-ridden women muttered to one another. "Why doesn't she come back?" But when she still didn't come back, they said, "She was only bad luck anyway." And with some relief they loaded their canoes and threw water on their campfires. They were well rid of the Raven Princess. For who could know? Perhaps she was being used by an evil spirit.

"Why doesn't she come back?" the aunt wailed

to her children. Moving with stealth so that the other women wouldn't see her, she placed a live coal in a clam shell and put it, with a piece of dried salmon, into the brush hut where Djoon would find it if she ever did come back. Then, sorrowfully, she too left the island.

From a screen of bushes where she had been watching the island's birds, the princess watched them go. No one had wanted her anyway. And to be as she was—a scavenger in the village—was a shaming of her once-great Raven Family. It was better to stay with the birds.

The island was alive with birds. On the rocky windward side, where the swells broke against the cliffs, puffins and cormorants climbed the air currents; sea gulls screamed and soared, watched by the eagles. On the gentler lee side, where the beach was, busy shorebirds ran along the edges, pecking into wet sand. And behind them, on the root-digging flats, great flocks of brant geese grazed.

There was something about the brants, Djoon felt. A warmth of belonging. "It's just the old story," she told herself. For once a Raven Prince had come upon a Supernatural Brant Princess swimming in her human form; and he had married her. But so homesick had she become that one day, when the geese were passing high overhead, she had put on her flying blanket and gone off with them. And so desolate was her young husband that her father, the Supernatural Brant Chief, had dropped a magical flying blanket down to him so that he could join them. Since that time, the Ravens had always felt a kinship with the brant geese. Indeed, the geese had once come to their rescue.

"Perhaps they will save me, too," Djoon murmured, watching them. After all, the future of the Prince's great Raven family now depended on her.

When the brants flew off suddenly with a thunder of wings and honkings, she began to walk slowy back to the brush hut. And after she had made a good fire from the live coal her aunt had left, she cooked the salmon. Yet, hungry as she had been, now she couldn't eat it. So she lay down in the lonely hut and went to sleep.

A thunder of wings and honkings woke her early the next morning. "The geese!" she murmured, feeling oddly comforted by their presence. Yet who could know? The most harmless-seeming creatures could be terrible beings in disguise; a floating log could be a sea monster. You couldn't know for sure about magic and witchcraft. You could only wait, terrified, to see what would happen.

She tended her fire and again tried to eat. But again she couldn't. Perhaps she, too, was to die as mysteriously as her family!

Guided by the chatter of the feeding geese, she made her way to the root-digging flat. But at her approach, the brants lifted and flew off.

Swallowing disappointment, the princess pulled up some grass at the spot where she planned to dig. And—amazingly!—the grass came up in a big turf, revealing part of a buried canoe. Throwing off more turfs here and there, she discovered that several large canoes had been buried, with mats covering their loads of dried salmon, dried halibut and oolichan grease. Who could have buried them? And why?

"How lucky I stayed with the brants!" she said as she lifted out some of the food. Yet . . . who could know? When she had replaced the mats and the turfs of grass, she carried the food to her fire. But again she couldn't eat it.

And so it went, day after day, until she became aware of something. She felt strangely light, as if she were more Spirit than body. Perhaps she was turning into a ghost? Then she noticed that the world around her seemed strangely bright; there was a radiance on everything. Strangest of all, now when she listened to the birds, she heard their cries and honkings only faintly behind Spirit voices.

"I am your Guardian Spirit," one of the voices said to her.

"The Raven Prince who turned into a Supernatural Brant!" she breathed, sensing that *he* was her Guardian Spirit. And *that* was why she had not eaten. Her body was being made light and clear for use by a Spirit Being. A wild joy surged through her.

Yet who could know? she thought. Perhaps she *was* only turning into a ghost as her body died of starvation. Seeming almost to float, she wandered about the island, always watching the birds, always listening to the Spirit voices.

One day, while there was nothing in her mind, she heard herself saying, "I wish someone would come from the starving village." And she found she was expecting the canoe that arrived next day from around a headland. Her body was indeed being taken over by a Supernatural Being. And she swallowed a moment of panic.

As soon as the canoe was beached, she showed the people the buried canoes and gave them some food, noting all the while how fearfully they edged away from her, as if they sensed that she *was* turning into a ghost. Then, directed by the Spirit that seemed to have taken possession of her, she said, "Now you must go back to the village. Take no food with you, but tell my kind aunt to come as soon as she can."

No one dared to make a murmur of protest. All moved with obvious relief toward the beached canoe.

Yet, when the aunt came, hers was only one of many canoes of starving women and children. And the air was so filled with birds that the people could scarcely see anything on the island; they could scarcely hear one another speak.

Then, above all the sounds of the birds, they

heard a wild, high singing. It was the Raven Princess singing; and they knew it for Spirit singing. Something strange and powerful was happening on the island. And who could know what it was?

When Djoon came to the beach and raised a hand, every canoe stopped where it was; every eye watched the princess. If the people had been fearful before, now they were terrified.

"My aunt's canoe may come in," Djoon told them in a voice that sounded strange even to her own ears. And only her aunt and her children dared to touch the island with their Eagle canoe.

"Take all the food you need," the Princess said, dreamily directing them to the buried canoes. Then she looked at the others, waiting offshore with awed, anxious faces. She noticed that several high-ranking ladies had painted their faces and put on fine robes for this visit to her; they had come in high-prowed canoes decorated with their Eagle or Bear or Wolf totem and paddled by slaves.

"I need two women to help with the singing," she called out in a voice that sounded strangely like a man's voice.

At once two high-ranking ladies stood up.

"No. Not you," the Princess said.

Others stood up, in turn.

"No. Not you," she said dreamily to each one in turn. Then she called for the two Raven orphans to help with the singing.

"You may all come ashore and camp," she told

the people in the canoes. And they all moved in with respectful awe. For who could know what was happening on the island?

Though she had given generously to her kind aunt, Djoon found herself by no means ready to give to the women who had treated her badly. "What can you offer in exchange for food?" she found herself asking in a voice strangely like a man's voice. And soon she had slaves to serve her and fine robes for herself and the two Raven orphans. She began to feel, once more, like a Raven Princess, though her voice seemed more like that of a Raven Prince.

She began to eat again, though most sparingly. And it all seemed directed by the Spirit that had taken possession of her.

Not more than a moon after the women and children had left the island with the food they had bought, Djoon felt moved to return to the village with the rest of the food and the buried canoes. She and her orphans sat regally in one of the canoes, with her slaves paddling and a cloud of birds around her.

At the approach of the princess with her soaring, swooping cloud of birds, the villagers gathered on the beach. Quiet with awe, they listened to the Spirit singing that rose above the crying of the birds. Fearfully they watched the now-splendid Ravens walk to where the carved cedar posts were all that was left of mighty Raven House. For who could know what Being now possessed the Princess? They watched her fan the carved cedar posts with an eagle tail. And they fell to the ground in terror as the house began to shape itself once more around the cedar posts.

"She has become a shaman!" people gasped to one another.

"A sorcerer!"

"A witch!"

Then they almost held their breath, watching her.

Her own eyes were now on the Eagle Chief and his daughter. For the golden tufts of tiny feathers decorating their heads had brought memories flooding. The wild canaries had come back? To flit like lively sunbeams through the alder and willow thickets along the river? Then she felt a wild rush of anger against the Eagle boys, who must now be stoning them as the Raven boys had once stoned them, to get the feathers. Then she caught her breath as she noticed how anxiously the Eagle Chief and his daughter were attended.

Indeed, the Eagle Chief and his daughter had fallen ill. And terrified that the mysterious sickness that had wiped out the Ravens had now come to the Eagles, people were filled with dread.

Every shaman in the village had begun to work over the sick ones with healing herbs and with wild dancing and a shaking of medicine rattles. Yet the two grew visibly worse. And full of terror and confusion, the people wondered if the Raven Princess had indeed become a witch and had put an evil spell on them. For who could know about magic and witchcraft? *Any* human or animal could be possessed by an evil spirit.

When the chief and his daughter were clearly dying, an Eagle delegation went to Raven House to ask for help. Knowing how little they had helped the princess, and fearing her revenge, they approached with anxious ceremony, to be met by the two younger girls.

"What will you pay the Shaman Princess to go to Eagle House?" the girls asked them. And it was quickly agreed that the Eagles should pay four slaves. After all, the Eagles reminded one another, the pride of the Ravens must be healed, too; there must be slaves to care for the great house and its high-ranking lady. Pride of family was one thing the confused people did understand.

Drums beat hypnotically in Eagle House as the two younger Raven orphans began their Spirit singing and the princess started her Spirit dancing around the fire. Watching her dance with her medicine rattle, alert eyes caught the movements of brant geese in her movements. And scarcely knowing what they did, they added the sounds of wild geese to the Spirit singing.

As she danced, the princess was listening to her Spirit voice telling her that it was indeed witchcraft. A witch had put an evil spell on the Eagle

Chief and his daughter as she had once put an evil spell on the Ravens. And the witch might be using the body of anyone, even a villager.

"Summon everyone in the village!" Djoon commanded, in a voice that was strangely like a man's voice. But when everyone had come, she said, "The witch is not here yet." Then she listened to her Spirit voice before she added, "Now the witch is coming!"

People almost held their breath, listening. But all they could hear was a strange birdlike whistling coming closer. A bird! Yet who could know? A witch could come in the guise of a harmless creature.

When the whistling witch came into the house, she did indeed come in as a harmless creature.

"A wild canary!" people gasped, watching the little bird with terrified eyes. A strangely large, strangely pale female wild canary, she filled the sudden silence with an unearthly whistling that was alarmingly unlike the usual cheery *tzee tzee tzee tzee setta wee see* of the sunny little songbirds.

"A wild canary!" Djoon breathed. And she remembered how the tiny creatures had risked the stones of the Raven boys to gather hairs around the houses before they had mysteriously vanished. *Then* she had thought that it was to line their small nests. But now she wondered. Had it had something to do with witchcraft? Certainly the mysterious sickness had started very soon after the hair gathering. She listened to her Spirit voice as she watched the canary.

Clearly caught now in a spell stronger than its own, the wildly whistling canary flew to a spot between the dying chief and his daughter.

"Tie her wings back!" Djoon commanded; and her voice was still strangely like a man's voice.

No sooner had the fearful people done this than there was a terrible noise outside, like the sound of a storm wind rushing toward the house.

"Those are the witch's children," the princess told the people. "Stop every hole so they can't get in!"

Before this could be done, angry little birds were pouring in, even through the smoke hole; they were flying fiercely about, pecking and clawing. People were cowering and trembling and covering their heads as the terrible little birds attacked them.

Then, as suddenly as they had come, they were gone. Only the first bird was left, sitting between the sick ones with her wings tied back. And now she was whistling a screaming, terrifying whistle.

The princess listened to the whistling. Then she said, "Now the witch is ready to let us break the spell that killed so many of my people and is now keeping these two sick. Untie her wings!"

When her wings were untied, the witch canary did not fly. Instead, she walked ahead of the

Shaman Princess and four chosen men, on and on at the edge of the woods until she reached a certain bush. Here she began scratching at the roots until she revealed a skull that had been buried there.

"A skull!" the men gasped. And when they had unearthed it with trembling fingers, they saw that it was full of human hairs.

"The hairs they gathered long ago from around Raven House," Djoon breathed, "and the hairs they gathered more recently from around Eagle House."

"That is how she worked the spell?" The four men marveled. Although everyone said that a bear's claw or an eagle's feather held the essence of the animal it was part of, to work *good* magic, no one had ever said that it—or a hair from a human!—could be used to work *bad* magic against the body it was part of.

"That is how she worked the spell," Djoon assured them.

"But WHY?" the stunned men asked.

"Because of the way the wild canaries' feathers had been taken," Djoon answered. Guided by her Spirit, she took the skull to the sea; and there she blew the hairs away in every direction. Then she watched the witch canary fly dolefully out to sea. "She is too shamed to go back to her tribe," she told the four men.

"Such a little thing!" the men said, watching the bird with awe.

"Such a little thing!" Djoon agreed, holding out one of her own hairs.

When they returned to the village with the skull, they found the Eagle Chief and his daughter walking happily about. And the Shaman Princess explained to them about magic and witchcraft. From now on, she told them, only feathers that had been dropped freely as gifts by the sunny little birds must be used for decoration; for the good-will of the birds must be in the feathers if they were to enhance the brightness of the wearers' Spirit selves. Similarly, an animal taken for food or clothing must be taken with appeasing cere-mony; for only then would there be good magic in it for the people who ate its flesh or wore its fur, claws or feathers.

At last the people understood about magic and witchcraft. And only one wily old sorcerer's eyes glittered with the thought that a hair from a rival's head could be put into a skull or a death box to kill him.

The once ragged, scavenging princess was greatly honored. And she in turn honored the brant geese. At a splendid feast, she danced the Spirit dance of the brant geese.

Then, one day, as the geese were passing high overhead, it was as though the Spirit of the long-gone Raven Prince left her to join his Supernatural Brant Princess. And Djoon became herself again.

First, she ceremonially adopted the two younger

Raven girls and presented them with high-ranking names of her family. Then she arranged noble marriages for all three Ravens. For she and the younger girls must have children—children who would be high-ranking Ravens like their mothers, in the way of these northern people of the West Coast. There must be daughters to carry the Raven bloodline. And there must be sons to wear the ancient chief names and bring back the pride of the once-great Raven Family.

THE TROUBLE WITH PRINCESSES was that often they were very hard on adventurous young men.

In the old fairy tales, they were always having to be rescued from dragons or giants or three-headed trolls. "Find the princess or lose your head!" the sultan told Aladdin after the lady had been whisked off to Africa by a wicked magician. This after having had to send the sultan "forty basins of gold brimful of jewels, carried by forty black slaves, led by as many white ones, all splendidly dressed" to win her in the first place.

Then there was the prince determined to marry a princess who had become the Enchanted Canary shut up in an orange. To find her he had to deal with a dog as big as a donkey, a red-hot oven, a strangling rope and a grinding iron gate, all before he came to a scorching desert. And after finding her, he lost her again and nobly agreed to marry a hideous girl who convinced him that she was the princess turned suddenly—and temporarily—hideous by a witch.

According to the tales collected in the New World, the princesses of the Far West could be quite as hard on bold, adventurous young men. There was, for instance, a princess known as Pretty One—if indeed she was a princess and not the granddaughter of the witch-woman who held her captive. The youth who tried to rescue her was not all that bold, it must be admitted, nor all that adventurous. But then, he had Lazy One to spur him on, and the remarkable "Little Fester."

4

Little Fester

It was in the time of long ago, when things were different. Then, the world was full of magic. And very strange things happened.

At this time, in a village far to the north, there lived a man known as Lazy One—with good reason, for he liked to do nothing whatsoever. And this made him most unpopular. For at this time, with a witch-woman killing one village youth after another, there were never enough hunters or fishermen or canoe-makers.

This witch-woman was holding a maiden captive in her camp up the coast from the village. Some said the maiden was her granddaughter. But others said she was a princess, captured from a faraway tribe. And, of course, wherever there was a rumor of a captive princess, there were bold youths who wanted to free her and marry her.

So it was in this village, until so many youths had mysteriously vanished, trying to free the maiden, that every hunting party, every fishing group, every canoe-making band was sadly short-handed. And a man as indolent as Lazy One annoyed the villagers.

Now one day Lazy One began to moan and groan and hold a wad of healing moss around one of his fingers. This finger, he said, was hurting beyond belief. He simply could not go to the mountains to hunt goat, he said, because it pained his finger to hold a spear or a bow and arrow. He couldn't help fell a cedar tree for a canoe, he said, because it pained his finger to hold a stone axe. He couldn't even go fishing.

"He has something in that finger," an old woman said to her husband.

"He has," her husband agreed. "And what he has in that finger is an excuse for not working."

But when the finger began to be red and swollen, even the doubters had to admit that there was, indeed, something in that finger. Yet, for some reason known only to themselves, the medicine men of the village refused to work over Lazy One. So he went about, moaning and groaning and holding up the sore hand with the good hand and, of course, doing no work whatsoever. If it was indeed an excuse he had in that finger, it was clearly a painful excuse.

As it happened, there was one youth who felt sorry for Lazy One. "You must do something about that finger," he said to the groaning fellow.

"But what can I do?" Lazy One wailed, holding the wad of healing moss around the throbbing finger. "None of the medicine men will help me."

"Then you must help yourself," the youth said. "There is certainly something in that finger that wants to get out. So you must hold it up under the smoke hole while someone pricks it from the roof."

"Hold my finger up under the smoke hole?" Lazy One wailed, looking up at the large hole that let the smoke out of the big cedar house. "How could I ever get up there?" He was no squirrel to leap along the poles that had been suspended from the roof for drying fish or holding fishing tackle.

"Leave that to me," the youth said. And while his friends placed a ladder and boosted the groaning fellow up, he himself stripped the branch of a thorn bush of all but one big thorn and climbed up on the roof with it.

Fearfully clinging to the ladder, Lazy One held up his finger, which was now as big as a giant's finger.

PRICK! The thorn pierced the enormous festering finger.

"Ooooowwwww!" yelled Lazy One, holding the wad of healing moss around the pricked finger as he tumbled down the ladder. Then he stopped yelling. For the throb had gone out of his finger, along with whatever it was that had popped out into the wad of healing moss.

Terrified of what might have been in his finger, he stuffed the moss into a covered box. And it was evening before he dared to open the box and look in. Then! What he saw left him standing with his mouth as wide open as his eyes. For there, lying on the moss, was a tiny man with tiny bright eyes looking up at him from a face no bigger than a wrinkled rose hip. A tiny man growing bigger every moment!

The curious villagers crowded about and looked at the tiny Being with mouths and eyes as wide open as Lazy One's.

"I must look after him," Lazy One whispered, as soon as he could whisper. And who could argue about anything as astonishing as a tiny man who had popped out of a festering finger? And having now found the best excuse ever for not going off with the hunters or the canoe-makers or the fishermen, Lazy One kept a constant eye on the little fellow. Now he had no trouble coaxing fearful women to bring food to him and his charge.

"Little Fester," everyone called the tiny Being. For it was as a fester in a finger that he had come to the village.

Little Fester grew with magical speed until he was as high as a man's knee and as lively as a squirrel. But as soon as he could run about, all he wanted to do was work! Day after day, there he was, chipping at a canoe log or painting a food bowl.

"It's because he came from a hand," people murmured to one another. "Perhaps all the work in Lazy One's hand had been waiting so long to be used that it finally popped out as Little Fester."

Perhaps that was true. And it would have been reasonable if Little Fester had simply done all the work Lazy One ought to have been doing for years. But he seemed to have put a spell on his indolent master, if indeed the bigger man was master in this case. Whatever Little Fester did, Lazy One had to do also. Which was even worse for Lazy One when Little Fester left off chipping and painting and began running races with animals before he hunted them with his tiny bow and arrows. Lazy One was always being found lying somewhere, panting from his latest exertions.

The villagers laughed in malicious glee and adored Little Fester.

"Now I know . . . why . . . I didn't like work," Lazy One panted one day to the youth who had pricked his finger. "And it's all your fault. You let him out. So now you must do something about him before he wears my feet off." He glanced anxiously at the spot where Little Fester was now making another arrow.

"What Little Fester needs is a real challenge for his energy," the youth suggested as Lazy One stirred himself to get up and make an arrow also. "Why not tell him about the captive princess? Now that he has raced, and beaten, all the animals around the village, he might welcome a real challenge."

"He might," Lazy One agreed, his eyes brightening and his muscles aching. "But if I suggested it, he would know that I was only trying to get rid of him. Why don't you suggest it?"

"If you like," the youth agreed. Indeed, so many of his friends and relatives had died trying to free the princess—if indeed she was a princess and not the granddaughter of the witch-woman—that he was more than willing to enlist the energies of someone as remarkable as Little Fester. So he spoke to the little fellow, keeping him from his work, which was very agreeable to Lazy One.

"Little Fester," he said, "a princess is held captive by a witch-woman."

"So I have heard," said Little Fester as he began to hop around the youth, looking at him from all angles.

"She is very pretty, they say, and wants to marry. But she can't find anyone she likes."

"Because the witch-woman likes them better, after she has cooked them," Little Fester corrected him as he continued to hop about, his eyes bright on the youth.

"As you say," the youth agreed. "Many youths from the village have died trying to marry Pretty One. Why don't *you* try?"

"Because I don't wish to marry," Little Fester told him, still watching the youth as he hopped around him. "Why don't *you* try?"

"Because I don't wish to die," the youth admitted. "They say the witch-woman always shows the suitor the strange dried skin of an animal and asks him to guess what it is. If he can't guess, she kills him. Perhaps . . . someone as clever as you could guess."

"I don't need to guess," Little Fester told him. "I know what the skin is."

"You know?" the youth asked, almost dizzy with the effort of trying to face the hopping fellow.

"Certainly. It's the skin of a louse, a louse she kept in a box and fed until it was enormous. And now that you know the answer to the question, why don't you go?"

"Yes," Lazy One urged. "Why don't you go? And take Little Fester with you in case you run into further questions." Now it was *his* eyes that were bright on the youth.

"Well. . . ." The youth considered.

"When you go toward her, go with the wind," Little Fester warned, as if it were all settled. "Don't let the wind blow from her. And don't go at all if a south wind is blowing. Go only with a north wind!"

"Well . . ." the youth said, swallowing.

"When suitors don't guess right, she kills them before she cooks them," Little Fester said, as if it were merely a fascinating fact. "But I don't know *how* she kills them."

"You don't?" said the youth, who was by no

means encouraged by all the fascinating facts.

"She won't kill you because you know the answer to her question. So even if I did go with you, I still might not find out *how* she kills them," Little Fester said, his eyes dulling with disappointment.

"Then again you might," Lazy One said by way of encouragement. "You never know with a witch-woman."

"No. You don't," the youth agreed, not at all encouraged.

"She has a large hot-stone box in which she cooks the suitors," Little Fester went on, brightening over that further fact. "But then, she won't put you into it, because you know the answer." Clearly, life could be very disappointing.

"You know the answer," Lazy One hastened to echo. "So go and free the princess and avenge the deaths of all the friends and relatives she has killed. . . . And take Little Fester with you," he added, as if he had just thought of that, again. "We both owe you that much."

"Well . . ." the youth said, spinning round now to keep facing the little fellow. "I would like . . . to avenge the deaths, and. . . ." And somehow he *had* to do what Little Fester wanted. "But . . . only . . . if you go . . . go with me," he stammered; for by now he was not only frightened, but also really dizzy from trying to keep face-to-face with the little hop around.

And so it was that Lazy One sank to the ground

in sheer exhaustion and relief as the youth and Little Fester started off up the coast in a canoe. "And if *a louse* isn't . . . the right answer to the question," he murmured, yawning, "let's hope she eats . . . Little Fester as well *azzzzzzz . . . zzzzzzz. . . .*" He began to dream a lovely dream about a witch-woman dancing about in pain as Little Fester throbbed in her scrawny finger.

🌿 🌿 🌿

WHEN THE none-too-bold adventurer and his lively companion neared the witch-woman's camp, a south wind was blowing.

"When you speak to her," Little Fester warned, "don't tell her about me. For that old woman has all kinds of dangerous things with which to kill people. And I want to find out what they are."

Feeling something less than cheered by his prospects, the youth waited until a north wind began to blow. Then he stealthily approached the camp. And there was the straggly-haired witch-woman gnawing on something he hoped was not a friend's leg bone. He gazed at her fearfully for some time before she glanced up and said, "Welcome, Grandson! From how far away have you come?"

Careful to keep downwind of her, the youth told her and also reluctantly accepted the food she offered. "I . . . wish to . . . marry Pretty One," he stammered.

She picked up a small box and took out a strange, dark skin. "What kind of skin is this?"

she asked the youth, looking over his juicy young body with her sharp, red-rimmed eyes.

"Oh . . . that's . . . that's just a louse skin, Grandma," he answered. And he trembled before the fury in her eyes.

"Where are you wise from?" she shrieked at him. "From your father?"

"Oh no," he answered, as casually as he could answer while beads of sweat gathered on his forehead. "Just from . . . from all around." Which was true enough; for whenever Little Fester had talked to him, it had indeed been from all around.

"Since you have guessed right," the witch-woman said, "you can marry Pretty One. But do you see that place over there?" Her scrawny finger pointed to where a rock rose sheer up from the sea. "A very large octopus—the Monster Devil-fish!—lives under that rock. I want you to kill it, Grandson." The glitter in her red-rimmed eyes told him that what she really wanted was for things to happen the other way around.

"Yes, Grandma," he gasped, escaping. And he raced back to Little Fester.

"An octopus!" Little Fester crowed, clearly delighted with the way things were going. "So that's the way she kills them, is it?"

"Yes. But . . . but I answered the question," the youth protested.

"And no doubt looked fine and juicy answering it," Little Fester chirped as he hopped around,

looking. "We'll kill the Monster Devilfish for her."
Indeed he was already fashioning a barbed spear
and looking about for a long stick to lash to it.

In much less time than the youth really liked,
they had launched the canoe and were peering
down through the water at the huge, hunched-up,
curled-up mass of devilfish on the rock shelf below. A den yawned blackly beside the rock shelf.

Fearful that—any moment!—the monstrous
tentacles would flail out and encircle the canoe,
the youth almost held his breath as Little Fester
made the thrust with his spear.

Then he sagged weakly in the canoe as the
triumphant little fellow pulled up the spear. *There
was a tiny octopus dangling from it!* A tiny octopus instead of the Monster Devilfish!

When they had paddled ashore, though, and
Little Fester had thrown the tiny octopus down
on the beach, it instantly became big again. It became a Monster Devilfish with gigantic tentacles
writhing madly to reach water.

"So *that's* the way she kills them, is it?" Little
Fester kept chuckling as he hopped about, looking at his catch from all angles. "Now, take it to
her!"

"Take . . . ?" The youth's mouth stayed open.

The little hop-around thrust the barbed spear
more deeply into the octopus. Then he pulled up
on the spear. And once more the Monster Devilfish was a tiny octopus, a tiny octopus dangling

from the end of the stick.

"Carry it on your shoulder," Little Fester advised, as if he were talking about an ordinary tadpole or minnow. "Now, be off to see what she'll do this time!"

The youth swallowed as he placed the stick on his shoulder. It was what the tiny octopus might do that frightened him. What if it suddenly became a Monster Devilfish again? With eight gigantic tentacles wrapping themselves around him! But he went off, as boldly as he could manage.

As he neared the witch-woman's camp, he tested the wind with a wet finger. Unfortunately, it was a north wind, so he had to keep going. And soon he could hear her clattering things about in her house. No doubt she was heating stones to drop into the big cooking box.

"Is . . . this . . . the Monster Devilfish you were talking about?" he asked, as disdainfully as he could manage, throwing it on the floor of her house as Little Fester had instructed. And the moment it touched the floor, the tiny octopus became once more the Monster Devilfish, a not-quite-dead Monster Devilfish. Its writhing tentacles groped fiercely about as they searched for water. Finding none anywhere, they finally flopped to the floor. And the Monster Devilfish became a dark, dead octopus.

"Where are you wise from?" the witch-woman shrieked as she danced about in rage.

"Oh . . . from all around," the youth said, staring fearfully at the gigantic dark, dead octopus. For what if it were not really quite dead yet?

"Take it outside!" the witch-woman screamed.

"But—" Yet the moment he dared to touch the stick and pull, the Monster Devilfish shrank; and he picked it up, swallowing. And the moment he threw it down on the ground, outside, it again became enormous. One giant tentacle lay near a big cooking box, where steam was already rising. Another lay near a cage-hut, where no doubt Pretty One was cowering.

"Do you see that cliff over there?" the witch-woman shrieked, pointing across the bay with a scrawny finger. "A Monster Rat lives there. When you have killed it, you shall have Pretty One."

"But I've answered the question," the youth protested, not knowing how long his good luck would hold. "And I've killed the Monster Devilfish."

"And now you shall kill the Monster Rat!" Such was the fury in her red-rimmed eyes that the youth was glad to escape, with or without the princess.

He rushed straight to Little Fester.

"A Monster Rat!" Little Fester crowed, hopping about in delight at the way things were going. "So *that's* another way she kills them, is it?"

"Yes. But . . . but I answered the question and killed the Monster Devilfish!" the youth protested.

"I knew she had all kinds of dangerous things with which to kill people." The little hop-around kept chuckling to himself as he started to do magical things to his small bow and arrows. "Come on, bold rescuer of princesses!"

"But I don't really want the princess," the youth said. "And I don't really want to go hunting a Monster Rat."

Nevertheless he went. And when they had discovered the rat's hole, they peered in and saw it asleep—a Monster Rat as big as a grizzly bear and no doubt twice as snarly.

It was three times as snarly, they discovered, when Little Fester's arrows had blinded it and they were trying to shoot an arrow into its fierce heart. Pouncing its way out of the hole, it snarled and lashed out and terrified the youth completely before Little Fester managed to shoot it through the heart. Then it stumbled into the sea. And they waited until the tide washed it ashore.

"Take it to her!" Little Fester said, hopping about in glee at the way things were going.

"Take it to her?" the youth echoed, dismayed by the size of the Monster Rat, as well as by the thought that it might not be quite dead. "How can I take it?"

"Like this," Little Fester answered, grasping the dead monster by its tail. The moment he touched it, it shrank to the size of a small mouse. And the youth had no choice but to carry it gingerly by the tail as he once again approached the witch-woman's camp.

Again he tested the wind with a wet finger. Again, unfortunately, it was a north wind so he had to go on.

"Is . . . this . . . the rat you were talking about?" he asked as disdainfully as he could manage, throwing it on the floor as Little Fester had instructed. As before, the moment it touched the floor, the shrunken monster became as big as it had been. Fortunately, though, it stayed quite dead.

"Where are you wise from?" the witch-woman shrieked as she danced about in rage.

"Oh, . . . from all around," the youth said, heartily wishing he had never laid eyes on the happy little hop-around, not to mention the witch-woman, the Monster Devilfish or the Monster Rat.

"Take it outside!" she screamed.

Trusting to luck and to Little Fester's magic, he touched the Monster Rat's tail. It instantly shrank, as the Monster Devilfish had shrunk. And the moment he threw it on the ground, outside, it, too, became enormous. Its nose pointed toward the big cooking box, where the water was now nearly boiling; while its tail pointed toward the cage-hut, where no doubt Pretty One was still cowering.

"I've done everything," the youth said, though still none-too-boldly. And he motioned toward the princess.

"Not yet!" the witch-woman shrieked at him. And indeed the poor youth went on to conquer a Monster Bullhead with terrifying spines, and then a Monster Crab with even more terrifying claws. While Little Fester continued to hop about in glee at the way things were going.

"I knew she had all kinds of dangerous things with which to kill people," the little hop-around kept saying to himself.

"But one of them might just happen to kill *me*," the youth pointed out as he resigned himself to taking the shrunken Monster Crab to the witch-woman's camp.

Again, everything happened as it had happened with the Monster Devilfish and the Monster Rat and the Monster Bullhead. And finally the Monster Crab lay dead on its back, outside, with one broken claw pointing toward the big cooking box and another pointing to the cage-hut.

"Now there have been four monsters," he told himself by way of encouragement, Four was the magic number. And he was heartily weary of his role as rescuer.

He looked at the witch-woman where she lay on the ground among her dead monsters, writhing in fury. "He has killed everything that belongs to me," she kept moaning, over and over.

"Everything?" the youth murmured to himself, much cheered by the news. "Except Pretty One," he called out above her moaning. "And I haven't even seen her." It was time he demanded something—especially since all her killers were dead. Though you could never be sure, with a witch-woman. "Except Pretty One!" he called out again, this time more boldly.

"Pretty One," the witch-woman echoed in a wild moan. "And the bracelet I lost in the sea." She looked at him, seemingly in despair. "Get the bracelet for me, Grandson, that I may have something to comfort me in my loneliness when you have taken Pretty One!"

"Well. . . ." The youth considered, for he was always more kind-hearted than sensible. "I'll get the bracelet."

"The bracelet?" Little Fester exclaimed, when he had heard all about it. "You should have demanded the princess. It's time you *demanded* something."

"Indeed it is," the youth agreed. "Get the bracelet!" he demanded.

"As you say," Little Fester agreed, too surprised now to hop around. And at once he began to dig for clams.

"But the bracelet is out in the sea," the youth protested.

"So are the fish who will find it for us," Little Fester told him. And for the first time, he seemed weary of the whole adventure.

When they had dug many clams and taken them out of their shells, they paddled out to a certain spot and dropped, dropped, dropped them into the water until a certain dogfish surfaced.

"Find the witch-woman's bracelet!" Little Fester told the dogfish.

The dogfish dived deep and soon returned with a gleaming copper bracelet.

"Take it to her!" Little Fester said to the long-suffering adventurer. And that was all he said. For, washing his hands—and indeed all of him—of the whole affair, he dived into the sea and swam away as a slender little fish.

"But! . . . But!" the youth called out after him. Then he swallowed several times, squared his shoulders and started off for the witch-woman's camp.

His heart almost failed him when he saw her again, writhing there among her dead monsters. But he lifted his sagging shoulders and went boldly toward her. "Here is your bracelet," he said, holding it out in a none-too-steady hand. "And now I demand Pretty One!"

To his surprise, and infinite relief, she got up and made her way to the cage-hut, cackling delightedly over her precious bracelet. She unbolted the door and called, "Come out!"

Pretty One came out. A maiden so beautiful that the youth was sure she must indeed be a captive princess and not the old woman's granddaughter.

"Take her!" the witch-woman shrieked. "You have taken everything else away from me."

"Except the bracelet," he reminded her as he

grabbed Pretty One's hand and raced her off to his canoe. He didn't really breathe freely until they were both safe in the village.

There was great joy in the village. Especially in Lazy One! For Little Fester was gone forever. Yet, fearful that he might come back, fearful that the people had been right when they had said that the tiny fellow was all the unused work in his hand, Lazy One began to go almost willingly with the goat hunters and the salmon fishers and the canoe-makers. Clearly a little work was better than a Little Fester.

As for the youth and Pretty One? They were married and might have lived happily ever after had it not been for Pretty One's temper. One day, after a heated quarrel, she sat down on a point of land and she vanished while her angry young husband was walking about to cool off *his* temper.

Vanished!

After all he had been through to win her! And after he had grown truly fond of her, in spite of her temper! Frantic with grief, he searched and searched the shoreline until finally, people said, he turned into a lonely beach snipe.

It's said that he's still out there, searching for the wife who, if she was indeed a princess, was a most troublesome one.

✿ ✿ ✿

THE TROUBLE WITH PRINCESSES was that sometimes they vanished.

In the old European fairy tales, there were the three princesses who vanished from a picnic; and no one knew they had been whisked off to the bottom of the river, where they were being guarded by a giant and a serpent with seven heads. There was Princess Rosalie, who had been carried off by the Invisible Prince. And then there was Princess Ingibjorg, who vanished from a forest and had to be rescued by Kisa the Cat.

Often the vanishing princesses were tricked into leaving their homes. The Princess of the Golden Roof, for instance, was lured onto a ship by Trusty John on the pretext of going to view fabulous treasures.

When the princesses of the Far West vanished, usually it was because they had been tricked. Usually they had been lured away by a Supernatural Being, who had come to them in the guise of a handsome prince.

One such trickster was Bogus, Chief of the dreaded Woodmen, who carried off the ghosts of drowned people. And since the princess he carried off was not a ghost, he wanted to turn her into one. Whether or not he succeeded will be found in "Bogus, a Ghost Story."

5

Bogus,
A Ghost Story

ONCE, IN THE TIME of very long ago, a princess of the Far West was in love with the prince from a neighboring village, and he with her. Their marriage had been arranged and was to take place at a great winter feast. But it seemed to them that winter would never come.

The totem pole villages of both prince and princess were in sheltered coves along the mountainous coast. But the rocky shore between them was often lashed by wild gales and pounded by the thundering sea. Nevertheless, so in love were the two young people that every evening the prince paddled to the princess's village to see her. Then he lingered so long before paddling home again, he could scarcely keep his eyes open next day when he was out sea hunting with the other young men.

"My son!" his mother warned him, "you will become so sluggish that you will turn broadside in a swell and capsize, or you will smash up on a reef. And Bogus will get you."

Bogus, as he well knew, was Chief of the dreaded Woodmen, who carried off the ghosts of drowned people.

"And when Bogus has taken you to his ghost village," the mother went on, "you'll never marry the princess."

"Perhaps . . . you are right," the prince agreed, yawning. And that very night he spoke to the princess about it.

"O mistress!" he said, yawning, "I must have a good sleep. So tomorrow I shall not come."

"O master," the Princess agreed, also yawning, "I'm glad we shall both have a good sleep."

Yet, next day, she was not glad. Every time she remembered that the prince would not be coming that evening, she sighed. And when evening came, her yearning for him was not to be borne.

Neither, it seemed, was his yearning for her. For she had not been tossing restlessly on her sleeping platform very long before she heard a rap on the wall, from outside. "O mistress!" the prince's voice wailed, "I couldn't sleep. Come away with me! Come with me if you love me!"

Without a second thought, the princess caught up a fur robe and slipped out of the big cedar house, out into the darkness, where the waiting young man led her to his canoe. Such was his haste to be gone, it seemed, that he didn't even touch her.

"O mistress! Come quickly!" he urged her. And she needed little urging. "Lie down in the canoe!" he told her. And she, anxious not to be seen by anyone who might be lurking about, lay down on a soft fur and covered herself with her robe. Now that she was once more with him, she relaxed into a dreamless sleep. She cared nothing for where they were going, as long as they were going there together.

She was awakened by the grating of the canoe on a beach. "Where are we?" she murmured. Peering through the darkness, she could make out the houses and totem poles of a village. His village, she thought.

Glancing at him, suddenly her heart skipped a beat. It *was* her prince. Yet . . . he made no tender move toward her. He spoke no word. And when he moved by her in the canoe, it was like the passing of a wind off a glacier.

Swallowing a vague fear, she followed him to the big house in the center of the village.

It was dark in the big, windowless house, and cold as a winter fog, silent as a frozen lake.

"Sit in the rear of the house!" he roughly ordered as he began to stir up the fire.

The princess hugged her robe around her as she made her way fearfully to the place he indicated. *He was not her beloved prince!* But who was he? Some dreadful being disguised as her prince? She almost held her breath as he moved away from the fire. But he went out and stayed out. And for the rest of the night, she huddled all alone by the fire. Where was she? And who had brought her to this icy place?

Morning brought further terror. For as the world lightened around her, the house began to fade away, as ghosts fade away in daylight, until there was nothing left but the smoldering fire. She was sitting on a grassy patch with the sea brightening in the dawn and the forest looming darkly against the mountains. All the houses and poles had vanished. Into silence. No sea gull screamed and swooped above the water. No raven cried from the forest. Only the lapping of the waves broke the deathly silence.

Shivering with dread, the princess stirred herself to find bits of driftwood to keep the fire going. Then she looked about for some means of escape. But there was no trail leading off through the forest, no canoe on the beach. There was no drift-log she might use with an improvised paddle. And there was no food.

Sunset found her huddled by her fire. Then, as she sat there, terrified of the coming night, houses and poles began to shape themselves, as though out of sea mist. His house began to come into view above her and around her.

Then he came in. Her prince! For an instant her

heart leaped. But he was not her prince. There, before her horrified eyes, he changed into a man as ghost gray as a frozen waterfall on a dark rock.

"Bogus!" she gasped. The Chief of the dreaded Woodmen, who carried off the ghosts of drowned people! But she had not been drowned. She wasn't a ghost. Scarcely knowing she spoke, she whispered, "No wonder you are cold as the wind off a glacier. You are cold as Death itself."

"O mistress!" he protested, in a voice that was only the hollow ghost of her dear prince's voice. "My heart is warm for you. That is why I have brought you to my village."

"Oh, no!" she gasped, covering her face with her hands, not to see him, for his eyes were strangely confusing.

"Tell me what you wish to eat, mistress," Bogus said, "for I'm sure you are hungry."

"I. . . ." She found herself looking at him and growing confused under his stare. "I. . . ." She *was* hungry, she remembered. "I . . . eat halibut at home." She wrenched her gaze from his hypnotic stare, for under its spell she felt herself growing foolish, muddled, unsure of what she said or what she did.

He went out at once. And the princess, alert to more trickery, followed to see what he would do. Shrinking back and avoiding his eyes, she watched him twist cedar withes before he plunged into the sea and disappeared into the night. After a time

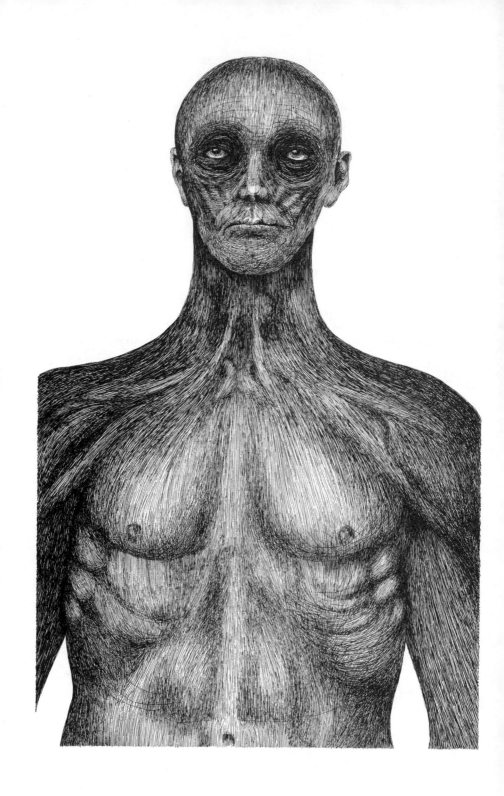

he came back, dragging four small halibut on his cedar withes.

"These you will cut and cook tomorrow," he told her as he threw them down on the beach. Then he went off into one of the houses.

Again the princess huddled all night by the fire. Again the house began to fade as daylight came, until there was nothing left. Again she was sitting on a grassy patch with the sea brightening in the dawn and the forest looming darkly against the mountains. Again all the houses and poles had vanished. Into silence. And this time her fire had gone out.

Busying herself to forget the horrors of the place, she searched until she found good mussel shells for cutting the halibut. Then she searched for cedar wood. And by chance she found a felled, split cedar tree with strips of its bark and poles lying on the ground. These she carried back to make a shelter. For the rains might come.

While she built the shelter and cut the halibut, she dried cedar bark in the sun. And this she rubbed until it was soft enough to catch fire. Then she shaved cedar wood and also made a fire-drill; and she drilled until fire fell from the cedar. By sunset she had a piece of fish roasting for her supper and the rest of the halibut drying by the fire in her shelter.

Before she had finished eating, the light faded and the houses and poles began to shape themselves, as though out of sea mist. His house began to come into view around and above her little shelter.

Then, when night had fallen, the man came into the house. But not into her shelter! For Bogus could not enter a house made by living hands. He laughed a ghoulish laugh and tried to compel her to look into his eyes. "Why did you make a house?" he asked. "My house was still there even though you couldn't see it. It would have kept the rains off."

"How . . . could I know that?" she asked, avoiding the hypnotic stare that made her foolish. In fright and confusion, she offered him some of the halibut. But he refused it in a hollow voice. Scowling about at her shelter, he turned and went off, as before.

For several days the princess ate the halibut, then huddled—terrified but safe!—in the little shelter. When the fish was gone, she began to grow very, very hungry. And one night when Bogus came to her shelter as usual, he said, "Now I will send you some salmon." This time, when he went off to get the fish, she did not dare to follow him.

Soon two young men came in carrying a strip of hemlock bark with a small roasted salmon lying on it. And as soon as they had left it on the floor at the door of her shelter, Bogus came.

"This time I'll eat with you," he said. And he seated himself just outside her shelter, with the salmon between them. Yet he made no move to eat. And much as she tried to avoid his eyes, the princess found herself caught in his hypnotic stare. She felt herself growing foolish, muddled, unsure of what she said or what she did. She was very, very hungry, she remembered. And the bright red salmon was truly enticing. In her hunger and confusion, she broke off a bit and ate it.

Bogus laughed his ghoulish laugh. "Thank you, mistress!" he said. "Now that you have eaten our food, you will become one of us."

"Oh, no!" the princess gasped. And glancing now at the roasted salmon, she saw that it was only rotten wood disguised as salmon. Hurling a piece of it at the fire, she watched the rotten wood smolder; and she shrank back from the frogs and lizards escaping from the skin.

All night she huddled in despair. And when morning came, the house did not fade away before her eyes; the village kept its houses and poles. Ghost sea gulls screamed and swooped above the water. Ghost ravens cried from the forest. She *had* become one of them.

Yet so great was her love for her prince, that her mind held strong against the terrible Bogus. She would not look into his eyes! She would never look into his eyes and give him power over her!

But now, she thought, no one would ever know what had become of her. And she watched the sea, not knowing what she watched for.

꙾ ꙾ ꙾

IN THE MEANTIME, her family and her prince were desolated. Search as they might, they could find no trace of the vanished princess.

Indeed, nothing might ever had been known about her had it not been for a young seal hunter from a neighboring village.

It was not long after her mysterious disappearance that this young man set out in his small, well-provisioned harpooner's canoe to hunt seals. And, of course, to look for any trace of the lost princess.

He had intended to hunt for some days. But he had not gone far before a thick fog came up. And paddle as he might, he paddled in vain; for he didn't know which way to steer. When night brought a strong wind, he rigged up a mat as a sail and let the wind take him where it would.

And so it went for several days, all day a thick fog, all night a strong wind. Then, at long last, morning dawned on a clear day. And he could see a pretty beach. So he went ashore and unloaded his canoe to air his provisions.

He had just carried his provisions to a spot where someone had recently built a shelter when he saw a huge wave thunder in. Before he could reach his canoe, the wave had lifted it, crashed it down again, and split it end-to-end.

He sagged to the beach in despair. Then, rallying his spirits, he carried the canoe pieces to where his provisions were, to strengthen the shelter. He kindled a fire and ate. And then, weary of coping with the fog and the storm wind, he lay down and went to sleep.

It was evening when he woke suddenly, feeling vaguely troubled. And there, all around his shelter was a strange mistiness, a mistiness that slowly shaped itself into a large ghostly house. He sat bolt upright and rubbed his eyes. But the house was still there, around and above him, growing clearer and firmer until it seemed as solid as his own cedar house.

"O friend!" a voice said hollowly from somewhere behind him. "I come to feed you."

Thankful for a voice in all this misty strangeness, the young seal hunter called out, "Come in that I may see you!"

A man came to the door of his shelter—an ordinary man, it seemed, in spite of the hollow voice. But he did not enter. "I will send you something to eat," he said, before he went off.

Almost at once the seal hunter heard a woman's voice call softly from behind his shelter. "Take care, master! Don't eat what he offers! He will send you roasted salmon that is not really roasted salmon. So only pretend to eat it, while really eating from your own provisions. Take care!" the gentle voice warned. "Or you will be lost as I am lost—forever!"

"You are the lost princess?" the young man

asked, in shocked tones.

"I am the lost princess. So take care, master! Or you, too, will be lost forever."

Two young men came to the door of the shelter carrying a strip of hemlock bark with a small roasted salmon lying on it. And when they had laid it down and turned to stand with their backs toward him, the young seal hunter picked at the salmon, pretending to eat it while actually dropping the bits into his lap and eating from his own provisions. When they thought he had eaten their food, the two young men went off.

"How did you come out, my dear?" the gentle voice asked.

"I did as you told me, Princess."

"O master, that is good!" the voice went on. "Listen now to what I must tell you. You have come to the village of Bogus by unlucky chance, as I came by trickery. And when he stares at you, it's to make you foolish. So, if you can't avoid his eyes, you must stare back, strengthening your mind against him until he looks away. I can't go into your shelter. But I can stay near you to warn you of danger. So listen to me, master, whenever I speak!"

"I will listen, Princess."

"Listen that you may live to return to your people and my people and tell my dear prince what has happened to me."

"I will always listen, Princess!"

Near the end of the troubled night, the seal
hunter heard another, deeper, hollower voice. "Are
you awake, my dear?" the voice asked. And there
was Bogus, standing at the door of the shelter.

Again, he seemed to be an ordinary man. Only
his eyes seemed extraordinary. They were staring
hypnotically at the seal hunter. But the young
man, remembering the princess's warning, stared
back, holding his mind strong until Bogus looked
away. Then it was morning. And the ghost chief
and his ghost house were fading into daylight.

And so it went the next night and the next,
while the seal hunter had more and more trouble
holding his mind strong against Bogus's stare. He
even began to wonder if it was the woman, and
not the man, who was trying to trick him. For
who knew who was the trickster in this awful
ghost village? By day he busied himself repairing
the canoe. But each night there was Bogus and a
growing confusion.

Each night the gentle voice reminded him not to
eat what they gave him, not to give in to the terrible stare. "I've heard what you've been saying
in your mind," the princess told him the third
night. "So I must prove it to you. Master, take a
bit of that roasted salmon and throw it on the fire
tonight!"

That night, the seal hunter threw in a bit of the
bright flesh the two young men thought he had
eaten. And at once it was rotten wood, smolder-

ing. When he threw in a bit of skin, frogs and lizards leaped away from it. "Indeed, it's as you say, Princess," he said in shocked tones. "Watch over me, mistress!"

Yet, later, after Bogus had been with him, he half-wondered if she wouldn't show herself to him because she was not truly what she said. And the princess saw his faith in her wavering. But again he threw bits of salmon into the fire and was once more convinced.

After the fourth roasted salmon had been dealt with and the gentle voice had called out to know how all had come out, he pleaded with her. "O Princess, let me see you! Let me tell your family and your prince that I've seen you!"

"Oh, no, my dear," the gentle voice moaned. "Since I've eaten their salmon, I've begun to look as ghost gray as a frozen waterfall on a dark rock. Now, you must be more strong-minded than ever, for Bogus is planning a new way to trick you. To-morrow a canoe will come, with men who will seem to be your relatives, as Bogus himself seemed to be my dear prince when he came to me. Take care, master! Take care that he doesn't trick you!"

"But what shall I do if I see my relatives searching for me?"

"First, ask them for their paddles. Take the paddles to your shelter and hold them over the fire. When you see what the paddles are, club them!

"Then take your canoe bailer, with water in it. Bite your tongue and spit the blood into the bailer.

Then, when you have asked your relatives to sit together in the middle of the canoe, sprinkle them with the bloodied water. And when you see what they really are, club them too! Then stab the canoe with your knife!"

"I'll do as you say, Princess," the seal hunter promised. "Keep watching over me!"

"I'll keep watching over you," the gentle voice promised. "But it's you who must stay strong in your mind, for they will all stare at you and try to make you foolish."

The night passed. Morning came with the fading away of the ghost village. And the young seal hunter was sitting in front of his shelter when he saw the canoe rounding a headland.

When it came closer, he saw that it was his father's canoe, with Killer Whale carved and painted on its high prow. And when he had run down to the beach, he saw that the people in the canoe were his father, a brother, and a brother-in-law. And as they all stared at him, seemingly in joyful surprise, he felt himself growing foolish. She could be wrong, he thought. For truly these *were* his relatives.

He wrenched his gaze away from them and didn't dare look at them as he called out, "Give me your paddles! Give me your paddles!"

He *knew* it was his father's voice that said quietly, "Humor your confused brother! Give him your paddles!"

Without daring to look into their eyes, he seized

the paddles and raced to the shelter. There he held one paddle over the fire; and at once it turned into a land otter—which he clubbed. The princess had spoken truly. And soon three dead land otters lay at his feet.

Strong once more in his mind, he picked up his canoe bailer with the readied water. He bit his tongue and spat the blood into the bailer. Then racing once more to the beach, he called out, "Sit together in the middle of the canoe!" And with his mind strengthened by what had happened with the paddles, he fixed his stare on his father's until the latter looked aside and said, "Humor your brother! Sit together in the middle of the canoe!"

The young seal hunter sprinkled them with the bloodied water. And as each man changed into a land otter, he clubbed it. Then he stabbed the canoe. And the canoe turned up at the ends to become a giant skate, which swam swiftly out to sea.

Stunned with the shock of it all, he staggered back into his shelter, where no Woodman could enter. The men in the canoe had been so utterly like his relatives that now he sat by the fire, shaking.

That night he heard the gentle voice saying, "They will try that again and again. And each time it will be more convincing. But hold your mind strong against them!"

"I'll hold my mind strong," he promised.

Yet, each day it was harder and harder. Each day he wavered.

Just before dawn on the fourth morning of the canoes, the gentle voice came to him. "O master, you have held your mind strong against Bogus and his treacherous land otters. Now be glad! For this time I think the canoe will be truly your father's canoe, out searching for you. But don't believe your heart, for Bogus has more tricks than I know of. Test the paddles as before! Test the people! Test the canoe! Then, if it is truly your family, go home with them. And go to my village with my good-byes to my family. Then go to my dear prince and tell him what's happened. O master! I can't come to you again."

Scarcely had she stopped speaking when Bogus appeared at the door of his shelter. And as the young man tried to outstare him in the firelight, he began to find his mind filled with confusion. Perhaps she was part of a more terrible trick, he thought. Perhaps now that she had convinced him that her words were always true. . . . Perhaps it was all a trick to make him frighten his family away when they did finally come. He wrenched his gaze away from the staring eyes. And as the ghost chief and his ghost village faded away into daylight, the young man sat scanning the sea in a confusion of hope and despair.

Then he saw the canoe. And truly this *was* his father's canoe, with Killer Whale on its high prow.

And there was his father, his mother, his two brothers, with his father's slaves at the paddles.

"Slaves of my son, paddle!" his father was shouting. "It *is* our lost one. PADDLE!"

The vigor of the paddlers almost lifted the great canoe from the water. And the joy of his family lifted the seal hunter's heart. Yet, afraid to believe his heart, he raced toward the canoe calling out, "Gather your paddles and give them to me!"

He saw the shocked look on his father's face, and on his mother's. Then his father's quiet voice was saying, "Gather the paddles and give them to him!"

"Stay in the canoe until I come back!" he called out, seizing the paddles and racing off to his shelter. In his excitement and wild hope that this was, indeed, his family, he held all the paddles at once over the fire. And they just began to dry off, as real paddles dried off. Yet, scarcely daring to hope that this was not some more devious trick, he tossed one of the paddles into the fire. And it caught fire, like true cedar.

But she had said, "Test the people!" So he picked up his canoe bailer with the readied water. He bit his tongue and spat the blood into the bailer. But what if his family should think he had become a madman? And leave him to the wilderness? "Test the people!" she had said. Yet . . . could he trust anyone in this awful village?

He rushed to the beach with the bailer and the

paddles. "Sit together in the middle of the canoe!" he said, still avoiding all the shocked eyes.

"Do as our lost one bids!" his father's quiet voice commanded. "Sit together in the middle of the canoe!"

The wildly hoping, desperately fearing young seal hunter sprinkled all of them with the bloodied water. And they stayed his family, looking at him with troubled eyes.

"Get more of the water if you wish," his father suggested.

It was his father. His wise, quiet father. Yet it could still be some terrible trick, he thought. "Test the canoe!" she had said. So he stabbed the canoe. And his knife stuck in the good cedar.

"You are truly you!" he cried out, trembling now with relief at his deliverance. "But this is the ghost village of Bogus, who has terrible powers. So let us leave quickly!"

At once the canoe was launched. And fear of Bogus sent it racing away through the water.

As they fled the pretty, lonely beach, the young seal hunter told them what had happened. Then he looked sadly back. "Tonight a ghost village will shape itself there. And a ghost princess—the ghost princess who saved my life. We must go first to her village, and then to her prince's village."

When they had done this and were back once more in their own village, they held a great feast.

And at the feast, the young seal hunter told the story of Bogus and the Vanished Princess. Then, shrouded with shredded cedar bark and with gray woolen fringes, he and his brothers danced a ghostly Woodmen dance.

And the princess?

Well, not long after her prince had heard of what had happened to his beloved princess, he did indeed capsize in a swell and drown, as his mother had predicted. So he, too, went to the ghost village. And perhaps—keeping their hearts warm for one another and their minds strong against Bogus —perhaps the prince and the princess lived happily ever after.

✲　　✲　　✲

THE TROUBLE WITH PRINCESSES *was that
sometimes they were spirited young ladies who
defied their parents in the matter of marriage.
They* would *marry the one they chose for
themselves.*

*In the Old World fairy tales, there was the
Danish princess who would marry Lazy Hans, and
the Arabian princess who would marry the
gardener's son instead of a prince. And then there
was the Fairest in the Land, whose many suitors
had lost their heads failing to accomplish the
impossible tasks her father set for them. When the
right suitor came along, she secretly helped him to
defeat her father's plan to kill him.*

*There were other princesses, too, who secretly
helped the favored suitor. There was, for instance,
the Magyar princess who, first, defeated her
father's plan to starve a Boy Who Kept a Secret.
Then, when he was sent into more lively dangers,
she actually led troops against a sultan to rescue
him.*

*So it was, too, with a spirited princess of the
Far West. After many suitors had died trying to
accomplish the impossible tasks her father had
set for them, she secretly helped the handsome
young man who had caught her fancy. Whether or
not she managed to marry him will be discovered
in the story of "The Fierce Eagles."*

6

The Fierce Eagles

It HAPPENED in the time of long ago, when narnauks
—the Supernatural Beings who could appear as
ordinary humans—had much contact with the real
people of the rugged wilderness of the Northwest
Coast.

At that time, one of the fiercest and most lordly
of the narnauks was Great Eagle, who lived at
Great Eagle's Nest on a small island far out at sea.
An island with only one gigantic, bony tree on it.

Now Great Eagle had a daughter who pined for
a husband. Although many suitors had come to
the island to arrange a marriage, Great Eagle had
always tested their worth in fierce tests designed
to kill them.

"I'll never have a husband!" Princess Eagle
screamed at her father one day.

"Not unless there's one worthy of you!" he
screamed back at her. And his fierce eyes were
flashing.

The princess sighed a furious sigh that was like a mighty whistle. She would never have a husband.

᙭ᙊᘓ ᙭ᙊᘓ ᙭ᙊᘓ

Now, AS IT HAPPENED, there was a human princess who also pined for a husband; though, in her case, the favored suitor would not have to prove his worth, nor even venture far to find her. Clearly a most suitable husband for the pining Princess of the Wolf Clan, he was already living in the same totem pole village, upriver from a thundering canyon.

The prince she pined for was the eldest, as well as the handsomest of the princes who were the possible heirs of their uncle, great Chief Salmon Eater. Indeed, he had been ceremonially named by his uncle as the next Chief Salmon Eater. And he was of the Eagle Clan; although, for some reason now forgotten, his family was not yet entitled to use the Eagle Crest on their house front, totem pole and other belongings.

"Why don't you arrange the marriage?" the princess stormed at her mother one day.

"The time has not yet come," her mother answered. For the princess was still young.

She was not too young, though, to see what was happening in the village. The prince was falling in love with his uncle's young, favorite wife.

"If you leave off arrangements too long," the girl reminded her mother, "*she* will be his wife!" For, as everyone knew, an unfaithful wife brought bad luck—even death!—to her husband; and on *his* death, the new young chief would inherit his uncle's wives along with his uncle's names and personal crests.

"A chief can have several wives," her mother reminded her, in turn. Clearly she was in no hurry to have her only daughter marry the rash youth.

"But I want to be his first wife," the princess said, blinking back tears of frustration. "And I don't want him to be the cause of his uncle's death."

Neither, as it happened, did his uncle. When he began to have startlingly bad luck in the hills, he knew that his wife was being unfaithful to him. And he intended to do something about it before it killed him.

Suspecting his beloved heir, he laid a trap and caught him. Then, in fury at this betrayal by his favorite nephew, and also in alarm for the future of a people led by such a rash chief, he had his slaves fill a hollowed plank with pitch, tie the prince to it, put the plank into a canoe, and set the canoe adrift in the river. There he would be rushed into the canyon and dashed to death on the rocks.

"You craved excitement," Salmon Eater muttered, though his tears fell.

Always alert to anything that concerned the prince she pined for, the Wolf Princess saw Chief Salmon Eater and his slaves set the canoe adrift. Suspecting what had happened, she roused the village. And such was the horror of the people that some talked of killing the chief. But after considering the outrage, after accepting the customary appeasement gifts from the now-anguished uncle, the incident was set aside. Salmon Eater was a good chief. And the prince-next-in-line would be a worthy successor. Indeed, they now admitted, he had a strength and steadiness lacking in his charming elder brother.

No trace could be found of the canoe or the prince. And only too soon the village seemed to forget all about him.

But the sorrowing princess did not forget. "He may have gone safely through the canyon," she comforted herself as she walked forlornly by the river. "And maybe . . . maybe some day he'll come back to the village." She would never stop hoping. She would never stop watching for him.

❊ ❊ ❊

Now, AS IT HAPPENED, the prince did go safely through the canyon. Held securely by the pitch, rather than by the cedar bark ropes the slaves had bound loosely about him, he lay stunned by the wild plunging rush through the canyon. At first he sensed only his swift passage down the turbulent river. But after a time, he sensed the great swells of the open sea. Then for several days, while the rain beat on his upturned face, he drifted.

He was faint with hunger when he woke one

morning to find the sun shining hotly and the canoe stilled. And when the sun had melted the pitch enough to let him move a little, he sat up.

He was stranded on a small island far out at sea, an island with only one gigantic, bony tree on it. And when he had managed to free himself from both pitch and ropes, he crawled weakly to the foot of the tree.

No sooner had he reached it than storm clouds began to race across the sky; gale force winds caught the canoe and dashed it to pieces on the nearby rocks. Somehow, he stirred himself to gather enough driftwood to make a rude shelter against the wind. Then, accepting his certain death, he went to sleep behind the shelter, while the gale spent its force.

By and by he was roused by a tiny but persistent poking at his back, and by a tiny but imperious voice saying, "You are invited, Grandson!"

"I must be dreaming," he said, glancing all about and seeing no one.

He felt a sharp poke at his leg. And there was a little white mouse looking up at him with her big, busy mouse eyes. "You are invited, Grandson!" she said again, as if she had been a haughty chief-woman instead of a mouse. Then she scampered off into a hole.

"I *must* be dreaming," the prince said, again. Nevertheless, he stirred himself to stagger after the mouse. And when he had reached her hole, he saw a trail winding off through the rocks. Following it in something of a daze, he came upon a large house standing out over the sea. The house was magnificently decorated with Eagle totems.

"Eagle!" he whispered; and his eyes brightened. He would find friends in an Eagle house. Yet he hesitated to enter. For there was something strange about this Eagle house.

After a time, a piercing voice called out from inside the house. "Come in!" it commanded. "Why do you stand there? Come in, son-in-law!"

"Son-in-law?" Almost before he could swallow his surprise, a man had appeared to lead him into the house.

A great fire was burning in the middle of the house within a white ring of broken clamshells. And on mats around the fire sat fierce-eyed chiefs and their people, all in the strangest robes he had ever seen. While a few had garments covered with starfish and mussels and abalone shells, most wore feathered regalia like the masks and mantles put on for an Eagle Dance at a potlatch feast.

At the rear of the fire, in the magnificently painted chief's seat, sat a big, fierce-eyed man in an Eagle garment and a headdress that was like the white head of a gigantic eagle. Beside him sat his wife, also in Eagle garments. And at their feet sat one of the most beautiful young ladies the prince had ever seen. Her cloak was of eagle feathers.

Perhaps he *was* dreaming, the prince thought. Or perhaps he had drifted out of the real world into the Spirit world. Or perhaps he was still in the real world of people and narnauks, and the talking mouse had been Mouse Woman, the tiny narnauk who was known to be the friend of young people in trouble. Realizing that his mouth was open, he closed it.

"We have been waiting for you a long time, son-in-law," the chief said. He indicated a mat that had been placed for him beside the princess.

As soon as the prince had seated himself, a feathered cloak was dropped around his shoulders, and bowls of seafoods circled the fire. Then Great Eagle spoke to the assembled people. "The prince is my nephew who has come a long way to visit me and marry my daughter," he said. "And now that you have seen him, you will always know him and help him!"

The guests murmured their approval as they finished eating. Then, in a sudden thunder of wings, they rushed through the smoke hole. As EAGLES!

Realizing that again his mouth was open, the prince again closed it. Was he indeed dreaming? If so, he thought, it was a splendid dream. For the maiden who would be his wife when the proper four days had gone by was the most beautiful he had ever seen. He gladly let her take his hand and lead him outside.

There Princess Eagle turned almost-fierce eyes on him and said, "You must know that you have come to Great Eagle's Nest. And you must not trust my father. He has killed every suitor who has come here. And he means to kill you. But *you* I will help." She smiled into his handsome face. "I *will* marry you! So I'll help you defeat my father."

Very secretively she replaced the feathered cloak he had been given with a seemingly similar garment. "There's much *power* in this Eagle Garment," she whispered. "Wear it, and you'll be as an eagle, but with the speed and strength of a whole tribe of eagles. And when you go out to hunt for food, I'll watch you from a tree, as an eagle watches. If you fly into danger, I'll help you. For I have mighty *Powers*." She took the other feathered cloak away to hide it.

Next morning Great Eagle greeted the prince as a chief should greet his chosen nephew and son-in-law. Then he said, "Perhaps you would like to try your wings this morning. The garment we've given you will let you fly as an eagle. My young men are out as eagles catching the whale I crave today. You might enjoy helping them."

"Indeed, I would," the prince agreed, though he had caught the warning flash from the princess's eyes. "I'll gladly help them." Indeed, he had often wished that he were an eagle, circling proud and high in the air, or shooting down, swift and sure as some immense arrow.

As he went outdoors, carrying the magical Eagle Garment, the princess followed him. "This is a trap to kill you," she said, turning fierce eyes on him. "But if you *will* try your wings, you must take off from the tree. Your Eagle Garment has great Power. And I, too, will help you."

When they reached the tree, they saw eagles circling out at sea, watching for the whale their chief craved. And eager to try his wings, the prince put on his magical Eagle Garment. At once he was an eagle, an awkward eagle lurching toward the tree.

"Eagles were not meant for the earth, but for the air," the princess assured him as she helped him up into the tree. Then, as an eagle, she perched beside him. "Once you have launched yourself into the air, you will be superb," she told him. "For the garment has great Power."

And so it was when he tried his wings. He was indeed superb. Exulting in his new-found freedom, he soared and swooped and climbed the air currents. And the rush of the air thrilled him.

"I'm an eagle!" he cried out as he perched once more beside Princess Eagle.

"With the speed and strength of a whole tribe of eagles!" she exulted with him. "Soon we will soar together!"

A sudden screaming of eagles out at sea caught their attention.

"A whale!" the princess cried out. "They've found a whale to tow to my father's beach."

It was a killer whale, with its black dorsal fin curving high above the sparkling water. And now the biggest of the hunting eagles had its talons fiercely fixed in the black fin. Another eagle clutched the first, with the others swiftly forming themselves into a chain of eagles to tow the whale; while the mighty whale flukes threshed wildly.

"They're in trouble!" the prince said. For clearly the plunging killer whale was about to pull the chain of eagles under. "I'll help them."

"No!" the princess screamed at him as he took off. "It's a trap of my father's!"

But the rash prince was gone. A Super Eagle, he felt the wild rush of the air as he swept high out over the sea toward the frantic wing beats of the struggling chain of eagles. Then his tilted wings sliced the air as he planed lower above the threshing, plunging killer whale; they folded as he hurtled down, then spread themselves to brake his fall as his big taloned feet thrust forward to grasp the highest eagle in the chain. And then, with the speed and strength of a whole tribe of eagles, he was leading the chain of eagles as they towed the killer whale safely to the beach.

"You have much Power, son-in-law!" Great Eagle called out as he came down to the beach. But the flash in his narrowed eyes showed little joy in the young man's prowess.

"I have much Power!" the prince answered; and the flash in his eyes showed defiance. The other eagles—now becoming men once more—gazed at him in admiration.

"With this garment, I can defeat your father's plans," he whispered to the princess when they were alone once more in human form.

"You defeated this plan only because I was sending supernatural help to you," she told him. "For that was no ordinary killer whale. You must never go off unless I am there, watching!"

The prince agreed, though secretly he wondered if indeed he had needed her help. He had surged with mighty Power in the magical Eagle Garment. Then he looked fondly at her. For she was truly a most beautiful princess, and she would be his in three more days.

Next day, though Great Eagle had plenty of whale to eat, he expressed a wish for octopus. "I crave a few rings from the tentacles of the Giant Devilfish," he told his chosen son-in-law. "But he has long defied my best hunters. Even you, son-in-law, with all your Power, could not take the Monster Octopus." He lowered his eyelids for a moment over a malicious glint. "And though I realize that your princely pride drives you to present superior marriage gifts, I think the gift of the Giant Devilfish is beyond even your powers." Now his eyes seemed to pierce his son-in-law's in challenge.

"I do indeed wish to present superior marriage gifts," the rash prince agreed, falling easily into the trap; for he *was* under the shame of offering no marriage gifts at all. And though he again caught the warning flash from the princess's eyes, he said, "I'll give you what you crave, father-in-law." As before, he picked up the magical Eagle Garment the chief still thought was an ordinary flying blanket.

And as before, the princess followed him out of the house. "You will indeed give him what he craves. Your death!" she almost screamed at him as they made their way to the rocky crevice below which the Monster Octopus lurked on a rock shelf close to his murky den. "This is another trap to kill you."

"I brought no marriage gifts to your family," the prince retorted as he stubbornly went on. He was carrying a long-shafted barbed spear well-lashed with holding rope. "I know how to take an octopus." For until he had moved into his uncle's up-river house to be trained as his heir, he had lived in his father's house at the coast.

"You may know how to take an ordinary octopus," she retorted, in turn. "But even with the Power of a whole tribe of eagles can you pull the Giant Devilfish to the surface when his monstrous tentacles are clamped onto the rocks? What if *he* pulls *you* into his den and clamps those tentacles around *you*? I beg you not to try it!"

"I brought no marriage gifts," the prince stubbornly repeated. Longing to feel, once more, the wild surge of Power, the exhilaration of battle, the rash young man readied his plan. And his eyes glinted with excitement as he peered down through the murky water at the huge, hunched-up, curled-up mass of devilfish lying on the rock shelf below.

As a man, he thrust the barbed spear into the monster. And the water blackened in the instant it took Princess Eagle to drop the magical garment on his shoulders. As a Super Eagle he rose, pulling at the writhing, flailing fury of tentacles below.

As the eight monstrous tentacles clamped onto the rocks, fierce talons tightened on the spear shaft, mighty wings beat the air. But pull as he would, he could not budge the Giant Devilfish. His heart pounded. His wings beat frantically. What if the monster made one sudden, spurting move and pulled him under . . . and flung the murderous tentacles around him before he could escape! His heart pounded. His wings beat frantically.

Then, suddenly, he seemed to surge with added Power. He felt the give on the spear shaft. Then he was lifting the flailing monster. And with one final burst of Power, he flew over the rocks and dropped the Giant Devilfish into a helpless sprawl of writhing tentacles.

Once more a man, the prince gazed at the monster he had conquered. "With this garment," he boasted, "I can defeat all your father's plans to kill me!"

"You defeated this plan only because I gave you

supernatural help," she told him, as before. "You must never go off unless I am there watching!"

The prince agreed, though again he secretly wondered if indeed he had needed her help. Then, as before, he looked fondly at her. For she was truly a most beautiful princess, and she would be his in two more days.

Leaving the Giant Devilfish dead on the rocks, they went to Great Eagle's Nest.

"Father-in-law," the Prince said, drawing himself up proudly, "the marriage gift you craved is lying on the rocks, waiting for your men to bring it to you."

Great Eagle's eyes flashed. "You have much Power, son-in-law," he said. And again the flash in his narrowed eyes showed little joy in the young man's prowess. Then he sent his men to bring home the food he craved.

Next morning Great Eagle asked nothing of his son-in-law. And the prince, feeling oddly disappointed, went out into the morning. Taking his magical Eagle Garment, he slipped off alone to the gigantic, bony tree. For he wished to test the Power he, himself, had in the wonderful garment.

No sooner had he perched himself on the tree than he saw a strange thing out at sea. "A giant clam!" he murmured excitedly. It was unlike any giant clam he had ever heard of. Floating with its immense shell open, it caught the sun on a mother-of-pearl lining more rainbowed and glistening than

that of the most precious abalone shell he had ever
seen.

"*There* is a truly magnificent marriage gift to
give him, unasked!" he gloated. And without one
anxious tremor, he swept out over the sea, a Super
Eagle with the thrust of a whole tribe of eagles. "A
truly magnificent gift!" he exulted as he circled
high over the opened shell.

"It thinks I'm an ordinary eagle," he told himself as the Giant Clam made no move to escape
into the cold depths. Then, with the speed and
strength of a whole tribe of eagles, he dived
straight at it. His immense wings spread them
selves to brake his fall as his big taloned feet thrust
out to grasp the top of the shell.

WHUSH! The monstrous shell snapped shut on
his feet. And while his heart pounded with fright
and his wings frantically beat the air, it began to
pull him under.

Then he felt a mighty eagle clutch him.

Princess Eagle!

Soon a chain of eagles was helping to tow the
Giant Clam to the beach.

There, instantly assuming human form, the
princess and her helpers smashed at the hinge and
pried the giant shell open. And at once the men
left them, content to have helped the great prince
who had helped them with the killer whale.

"It's a marriage gift I can present, unasked," he
defiantly told the princess; though he quaked in-

wardly under her fierce eyes, and his feet throbbed with pain.

"A gift you can present only because I helped you," she screamed at him. But her hands were gentle on his injured feet as, with a few strange movements, she healed them.

"But it is a magnificent gift!" he insisted, gloating over the immense expanse of precious, rainbowed mother-of-pearl. "As it should be for you." He looked so fondly at the princess, who would be his in one more day, that her fierce eyes softened.

"A magnificent gift!" she agreed. Indeed, it would be treasured as decoration on countless robes and headdresses and inlaid wealth chests; it would glisten on many high-ranking ears.

"And it *was* unasked," he went on, surging with pride in the gift.

"Was it?" she challenged him. "This was yet another trap of my father's to kill you. And once again you would not have defeated him if I hadn't helped you."

"True," the prince admitted. And he swallowed at the thought that there might yet be one more hazardous test of his worth. On the fourth day.

After the prince had presented the glistening gift to Great Eagle, the princess drew her father aside. "You can do nothing against his Power," she told him, saying nothing about the magical Eagle Garment and the other supernatural help she had given the rash young man. "Why will you try to kill this suitor when you know that I want him for my husband? If you *did* manage to kill him, you would lose not only a handsome and valiant son-in-law; you would lose your only daughter!" And so fiercely did she glare at him that Great Eagle finally lowered his own fierce gaze.

"I will do nothing further to kill him," he promised. "Indeed, I will adopt him as my beloved nephew and present him with the greatest of Eagle Crests."

"If a fourth test is needed," she went on, "I have one of my own in mind."

And so it was that on the fourth day Great Eagle greeted the prince as a chief should greet his chosen nephew and son-in-law. With much ceremony, he gave his daughter and his own magnificent Eagle Crest to the prince.

"Now our troubles are over," the prince said to his beautiful wife.

"Are they?" she challenged. For she was wiser than he was.

"They are," he assured her. And for a time they were very happy.

For a time, the prince was supremely happy. Not only had he a beautiful and loving wife, he also had the speed and strength of a whole tribe of eagles as he swept out with her from the gigantic, bony tree. Circling high over the waters and shooting down like some immense arrow, he gloried in a wild freedom he had never before known.

Then he began to wish he could present the long-coveted Eagle Crest to his family. He began to be lonely for his relatives and his friends. He began to long for the old life of the village and the river and the hills where he had hunted.

"What's the matter with my son-in-law?" Great Eagle asked his daughter.

"He longs for his people and his village," she told him, sighing.

"Then you must take him back to them," her father said, surprising her by his readiness to have them go.

Perhaps he was wiser than she was? she thought, frowning.

And so it was, soon after, that the prince and the princess flew off from the gigantic, bony tree on the small island far out at sea. For days they flew, resting now and then on a rock or an island. And the prince found his eagerness rising when they reached the river, and then when they sailed high above the canyon where rushing white waters hurled themselves against rock.

There's my uncle's house!" he called out, indicating the biggest house in the center of the row of big cedar houses along the river. And his eagle eyes flashed to think that soon it and its totem pole would be entitled to wear the most magnificent of all Eagle Crests. He would be a hero to the people, he thought, a subject for the storytellers. Chief Salmon Eater would lavish gifts and honors on him to wipe out his own cruel deed.

"We'll light on his roof!" he cried out. And with the speed and strength of a whole tribe of eagles, he circled high above the house, then shot down like some immense arrow. His great wings spread themselves to brake his fall as his big taloned feet thrust out to land on the roof. He had come home. And Princess Eagle had come with him.

"Eagles!" the villagers gasped, watching the splendid arrival.

"Those are no ordinary eagles," the chief said. And his raised hand stayed any hasty arrow. Now he seemed a weary old man. For nothing had gone well with him since he had set his beloved heir adrift in a canoe on a pitch-filled hollowed plank.

All watched with wondering eyes as the two great eagles took off. They were still talking excitedly about the mighty birds when the long-lost prince and his wife walked into the village.

The prince had returned!

He had not been dashed to death in the canyon!

He had returned with a beautiful wife!

Agog with excitement over the mysterious return of the prince they had given up for dead, the villagers gathered in his uncle's house to hear his story, celebrate his return, and welcome his wife, who was clearly a lady of high rank.

After he had told his story, the prince proudly presented the greatest of all Eagle Crests to his uncle and the people of their family. And there was much rejoicing in the village.

❄ ❄ ❄

"HE HAS COME BACK, as I knew he would," the Wolf Princess said to her mother; and her eyes were shining. For one glance at the young man she had always pined for had brought all her old longing for him racing through her.

"But he has a wife," her mother protested, looking at her daughter with anxious eyes.

"A chief can have several wives," the daughter reminded her. "And he will be a great chief—a chief entitled to display the most magnificent of all Eagle Crests on his house and pole and all his belongings." Though the returned prince did not seem to have noticed her, she planned to bring herself to his attention as soon and as secretly as possible.

"But we are already arranging your marriage with the prince-next-in-line," her mother protested. "He is a most worthy prince. And he loves you."

"Nevertheless, it is Salmon Eater's heir I will marry," the Wolf Princess defiantly stated. And she began to plot her escape from her ever-hovering attendants.

For a time the prince settled very happily into the life of the village and the river and the hills where he hunted. Avoiding his wife's flashing eyes, he turned his mind firmly away from a longing for the wild joy of flight. And he kept away from his uncle's young, favorite wife, though he still felt the old attraction. For he was enjoying his new importance.

Also, he was more than a little in awe of Princess Eagle. It was this awe that made him do her bidding about one strange and often repeated request. Though it was really slave's work, he always fetched a special dipper of water for her from a certain stream near the village. And if he always wondered why she took a particular white eagle feather from her hair and dipped it into the water, she always smiled so fondly at him after the dipping that he pushed away the thought that it was some sort of test.

One evening, when he went to fetch his wife's water, he found the Wolf Princess alone at the stream. And since she was a beautiful young lady who had been flashing eager glances at him ever since his return, he happily lingered with her. Soon he was embracing her.

"I've always loved you," she confessed. "I've always intended to marry you. But you have a wife."

"A chief can have several wives," he reminded her. "I will soon be a chief and marry you, too." And after embracing her warmly again, he asked her to meet him at the stream the next evening. As he left her, his eyes were bright with excitement. For life in the longed-for village had not proved quite as exciting as he had expected. Too, there were those who made scornful remarks about the way he fetched his wife's water. "Are you her slave?" they had teased him.

The teasing had irked him. Well, he would not be in awe of his second wife; and the thought was pleasing to him. In fact, he wondered why he had never really noticed the Wolf Princess before he had left the village; for there had been talk of arranging a marriage for them. But then he had been enamoured of his uncle's young, favorite wife, who also was now waylaying him, though so far without making him dare to be unfaithful to Princess Eagle, who might well tear a rival to pieces.

He took the dipper to her. As always, she took the particular white eagle feather from her hair and dipped it into the water. But this time, instead of smiling fondly at him, she glared fiercely at the water. And when he, too, glanced at it, he saw that now there was a murkiness.

"You're unfaithful to me!" she screamed at him.

"That's what you were testing?" he retorted.

"That's what I was testing. An eagle has one mate. And I will not share you with anyone. Not with your uncle's wife, who looks at you with unconcealed yearning. Nor with the Wolf Princess, who escaped from her attendants this evening. If you must have many women, you will not have me." With one fierce flash of her eyes, she picked up her Eagle Garment. And then she was gone, thrusting off into the bright western sky as a Super Eagle.

Almost without thinking, the Prince picked up

his magical Eagle Garment. And with the speed and strength of a whole tribe of eagles, he followed her to a rocky pinnacle.

"Go with the woman you want!" she screamed at him.

"I will go with the woman I want!" he screamed back at her. For now that he had felt his wings again, he knew how fiercely he had longed to soar and dive and sweep out over the sea. If he were to stay in the village and become a chief, he knew he must learn to send others out adventuring while he devoted himself to the welfare of the people. He must forego forever the wild excitement of flying with a fierce-eyed but glorious mate.

※ ※ ※

THE WOLF PRINCESS watched him go off into the splendor of the western sky. This time, she knew, he would never come back. The young man she had always pined for had flown out of her life forever. And as though a dark spell had been broken, she felt a surge of release.

Then the prince-next-in-line was standing with her. And the certainty of his love warmed her. Glancing at him now, she saw that he was more handsome than she had realized. And soon he would be Chief Salmon Eater, a chief entitled to display the greatest of all Eagle Crests. She smiled briefly at him before she went off to her mother.

"Why don't you arrange the marriage at once?" she quietly suggested.

"But . . . you said . . ." her mother protested.

"I said it's Salmon Eater's heir I will marry," the princess reminded her mother. "And the new heir will not be so flighty." The tears she blinked back were not all tears of sadness.

Indeed, as it happened, now both princesses became happy. And they, like the prince who had given his people the coveted Eagle Crest, would be remembered forever by the old storytellers.

THE TROUBLE WITH PRINCESSES was that they had to marry the prince or the five-headed troll they were told to marry.

In the old European fairy tales, many of them were meek young ladies who ate sugarplums and did what was expected of them. There was, for instance, the princess who let herself be married to the Enchanted Pig because it was clearly her fate to marry the pig; and besides, the king thought that he might not really be a pig.

But there were princesses who were not so meek. There were runaways like Princess Mayblossom. Shut up in a tower to keep her safe until her twentieth birthday, she not only escaped from the tower, she also ran off with her destined prince's handsome-but-worthless ambassador, Fanfaronade.

Among the princesses of the Far West, there seemed to be few meek young ladies. Perhaps the vigorous outdoor life of these princesses made them unusually spirited. Or perhaps it was only the stories of the venturesome ones that were told, because the trouble such princesses got into was expected to discourage other defiant young people. Certainly there was little in "Song of the Bears" to encourage further defiance in the matter of marriage.

Even Mouse Woman—the wonderful little narnauk who was a friend to young people in trouble—could not have helped runaway Princess Kind-a-wuss, because what she was doing was not a proper thing to do. And this "Good Fairy" of the Northwest Coast was a most proper little Being.

7

Song of the Bears

IT HAPPENED in the time of very, very long ago,
when things were not as they are now on the big
offshore islands of the Haida, the haughty Lords of
the Coast.

Then, sharing the forested islands with the people and the animals, were the Myth People, who
were not truly people, yet not truly animals either.
And the most troublesome of these were the Bear
People, who could appear as humans or as bears.
What made them troublesome was that sometimes
the Bear People wanted to marry real people.

So it was at one time with the handsome Prince
of Bears. He yearned to marry a human princess.
So, wandering the vast green wilderness, he
stealthily watched human princesses until he
found the most beautiful of all, Kind-a-wuss. "I
will marry her," he told himself. And his heart was
filled with yearning.

※ ※ ※

Now, AS IT HAPPENED, this was not the only trouble that threatened Princess Kind-a-wuss. There was also a problem about her proper marriage to a human prince. For the marriage of the princess was all important to the people of her Raven Clan. It would be her sons who would become the great Raven Chiefs; and their father must be worthy of them. Rank and bloodline were carefully guarded by the haughty Haida, who had two bloodlines: Eagle and Raven.

The proper husband for her was, of course, the Eagle Prince. For a man and his wife must never be of the same totem, or crest. Children belonged to their mother's totem, and those children must marry someone from the opposite bloodline. Just as her Raven mother had married an Eagle Chief, so the Raven Princess must marry an Eagle Prince.

The trouble was that Kind-a-wuss loved a youth who was neither Eagle nor prince. Not only was he a commoner, he was a Raven commoner. And people could gossip of little else than the princess's love for the youth who had been her friend since childhood.

"They should have stopped the friendship long ago," they said, meaning both sets of parents; though they themselves had always delighted in the friendship.

"The princess will always be safe with Quiss-an-kweedass nearby," they had always said, as indeed the parents, too, had said. For Quiss-an-kweedass was a handsome and daring youth.

Though he would never be allowed to captain one of the mighty sea-going canoes, his skill and daring on sea hunts and slave raids delighted the haughty Haida. And clearly he would die for the princess. "She will always be safe with him nearby," they had said, over and over.

Now, however, when the two young people had reached the age for marrying, and when their friendship was clearly blossoming into love, they said other things. "Does Quiss-an-kweedass forget that the princess is as high above him as he is high above the slaves?" they said. The slaves were not Haida; they were aliens who had been captured from tribes along the coast.

But the difference in their rank was by no means the worst of it. "They are both Ravens!" people gasped to one another, though there was little need to remind anyone.

Always, this had been the most terrible thing young people could do—marry someone from their own crest. Indeed, there were dreadful stories of young people who had been impaled on sharpened stakes or staked out in the sea to let the rising tide take them in punishment for what was regarded as incest. For didn't *all* Ravens trace back through their mothers to the great woman who was their common ancestor? Whatever their rank, Ravens were brothers and sisters.

"The parents must do something," people said, "before it's too late."

Indeed, the parents were saying the same thing.

"We must do something," they were saying. "We must marry them off to the proper people. At once!"

"It's all arranged," the Eagle Chief and his Raven wife told their daughter. "You will marry the Eagle Prince."

"I will marry no one but Quiss-an-kweedass," the spirited Princess told them. "The Eagle Prince has no wish to marry me, either." It had long been clear that *he* loved one of the noble Raven girls who were her friends and attendants.

"Perhaps you'll change your mind when you've been imprisoned for a time," they told her. And while preparations went on for her marriage, she was placed in a guarded room in her father's Eagle House.

It was the same with the youth she loved.

"It's all arranged," his parents told him, after an anxious conference with the Raven Chief. "You will marry the Eagle girl we've chosen for you."

"I will marry no one but Kind-a-wuss," he told them. For he, too, was spirited.

"Perhaps you'll change your mind when you've been imprisoned for a time," they told him. And at once he was placed in a guarded room in Raven House.

Maybe it was the Eagle Prince and the Raven attendant he loved who helped them. However it was managed, it was not long before the two young prisoners escaped.

The word raced through the village.

"They've gone!" people gasped to one another.

"What will happen now?" they asked one another. For surely the lovers would be found and punished.

"Will they be impaled on sharpened stakes?"

"Or staked out for the rising tide to take them?"

Then, as time passed and the two had not been found, the questions changed. "What's happened to them?" people asked. "Have they perished in the mountains . . . or been drowned crossing a river?"

At last the hunters stopped searching for them.

Now, AS IT HAPPENED, the lovers had not perished in the mountains. Nor had they been drowned crossing a river. Instead, they had made their way through the wilderness and across a river on a driftlog. And they had finally reached a spot where no one would find them. There they had built a hut —the rudest of huts, for they had escaped with nothing but their two knives. "Here we can be happy together," they had told one another.

Wrapped up in their own concerns, neither sensed the hovering presence of the Prince of Bears, who still yearned to marry the beautiful human princess.

For a time they were very happy.

Then the youth began to worry about the princess. "At home you would have women and slaves to serve you," he said as he anxiously watched her cut the fish he had caught with an improvised net.

"At home I would not have you," she told him, holding a cut finger as she smiled wearily at him.

"You'd have elegant bowls to eat from," he went on, glancing at their hastily-made wooden dishes, "fine robes to sleep under, and a good roof when the gales come. You'd have no concern for the food in the storage boxes."

He must improve the hut before the winter gales came, he knew. He must hunt and fish to have dried stores, yet also help Kind-a-wuss to gather berries and roots and firewood. There was too much to do without proper equipment!

What he knew was that he must slip back to the village for tools. What he didn't know was that the Prince of Bears was stealthily watching his every movement. And the princess's.

Determined to slip back into the village for his stone axe and other equipment, he worked night and day to be sure the princess would not suffer during his absence. Then he told her he was going.

"Oh, no! They'll catch you!" she protested, clinging to him. And when she couldn't turn him from his purpose, she said, "I'll go with you."

"No. It's better that I go alone."

At least she would go partway with him, she insisted. And she did indeed set off with him.

"Now you must go back!" he said when they came to the river. "You must stay at the hut. Promise me!"

"I'll stay at the hut," she promised. And almost blinded by her tears, she watched him cross the river and go on his way. Then she turned sadly back toward the lonely little hut.

But she was weary from unaccustomed hard work. She was desolate at his going. So, when she reached a mossy bank under a sheltering tree, she threw herself down on the moss and sobbed herself to sleep. All unaware of the bear eyes watching her.

As Quiss-an-kweedass went on his way, a strange uneasiness began to fill his heart and mind. "I'm so used to taking care of her, I think she can't take care of herself," he muttered. Yet . . .

"The faster I go, the sooner I'll be back," he told himself. And he raced on toward the village.

He entered the house with stealth, at night, and silently gathered up the equipment he needed. Yet his parents heard him.

"My son!" his mother said, rushing to embrace him. "Where's the princess?"

Frantic to be gone, Quiss-an-kweedass whispered his story. "I must race back to her," he said, pulling away.

But now his father was holding him, firmly, by both arms; he was fiercely saying, "No! You've brought nothing but disgrace to your family and her family. You'll not escape again!"

"But. . . . If I don't return, Kind-a-wuss will perish."

"If you don't return, Kind-a-wuss will come back to find you here."

"And what will she find here?" the youth stormed at his father.

By now, other strong hands were on him. And soon he was once more imprisoned, this time more securely.

Yet once more the desperate youth escaped. With little of the equipment he had come for, he raced frantically toward the hut. Would all the food be gone? And the firewood? Would Kind-a-wuss be starving?

Finally he reached the hut.

And she was not there. After a few frantic glances around, he knew that she had never been there since the morning they had both left. What had happened to her?

Perhaps she had lost her way, returning. Desperately hoping to find some trace of her, he searched up and down the river, through the timber. Calling her name, he went up into the mountains.

"Kind-a-wuss!" he cried out.

"Kind-a-wuss!" the rocks echoed. And then there was silence. A horrifying silence. The princess was dead.

After frantic days of searching, he knew he must rouse the village to find her. And as he raced back once more to the village, an anger grew in him. If his parents had not held him prisoner! If he and Kind-a-wuss had not been imprisoned in the first place!

"Kind-a-wuss is lost!" he cried out fiercely as he ran into the village. And the people gathered around him with frightened faces.

"Send out the searchers!" he implored them. "Do what you will with *me*! After you have found *her*!"

"The fathers are going," women whispered to one another as the searchers readied to go at once. So perhaps the young people would not be impaled on sharpened stakes, after all, or staked out in a rising tide. "Quiss-an-kweedass was always a fine youth," they reminded one another, recalling his skill and daring at sea. "And the princess was well-loved."

Quiss-an-kweedass led the search party with desperate energy. But search as they would, they could find no trace of the vanished princess.

"We must go home now," the Eagle Chief said after ten days. And there was pity in the eyes that gazed around the poor little hut where his daughter had tried to be happy. She had indeed been punished for the terrible thing she had done. And now he would give a great Potlatch Feast, with lavish gifts, to lift the shame from his house and from the rejected Eagle Prince.

Quiss-an-kweedass had no choice but to return to the village. Forlornly he picked up a hair tassel the princess had worn on the night they had both escaped. Putting it sadly into his pouch, he went back with the others to the village where now, trying to drown his grief, he became even more daring than he had been on the sea hunts and the slave raids.

Days passed into seasons, and seasons into years. Now, when Kind-a-wuss was mentioned, it was only as a beautiful girl who had been lost and never found. Even the Skaggies—the medicine men who went on spirit journeys—had not been able to discover anything. Clearly the princess was dead. And people seemed to forget her.

Quiss-an-kweedass never forgot her. He could not believe she was dead. Somewhere, somehow, she was alive; and somewhere, somehow, he would find her. He carried her hair tassel with him always, wetting it at times with secret tears.

Then one day he heard of a Skaggy who lived at some distance from the village, a Skaggy with exceptional powers of clairvoyance, people said. So at once he set off to see him, taking a handsomely woven blanket as payment for services.

This Skaggy was even more scrawny than most of the medicine men, his long hair more straggly. And his eyes burned more fiercely with visions of what mortal men do not see.

"Have you anything belonging to the princess?" he asked the young man, staring at him with his piercing eyes. And when he had held the long-treasured hair tassel for a while, he spoke in a strange, unearthly voice. "I see a young woman lying on the moss," he said, looking back through time. "She seems to be asleep. . . . It is Kind-a-wuss."

Almost holding his breath, the young man waited for the Skaggy's next words. "There is something in the forest, coming toward her."

Quiss-an-kweedass held his breath, waiting.

"It is a large bear. . . . He takes hold of her."

Quiss-an-kweedass let out his breath. He fixed his eyes on the Skaggy's and waited.

"She struggles to get away from him. But he is too strong. And he has been yearning for her for a long, long time." The Skaggy's eyes were burning with his vision of what had happened. "He takes her through the forest. . . . Now I see a lake. They stop at a cedar tree by the lake. There is a raised house behind the cedar tree." For a while, the unearthly voice was silenced. Then it continued. "Now the bear is like a man. A handsome young man!"

"The Bear People!" Quiss-an-kweedass gasped. And his eyes stayed on the old man's.

"I see her . . . now!"

"Still alive!" Quiss-an-kweedass murmured. "She's still alive!" His eyes brightened on the old man's.

"She lives in the raised house behind the cedar tree," the Skaggy went on. "She has been there for a long, long time. And her eyes are sad eyes. . . .

Yet they brighten when they glance at her two children."

"Children?" The young man swallowed.

"If you go to the lake and find the cedar tree, you will find Kind-a-wuss."

"How will I find the lake?" The young man's voice was eager.

"I will take you there," the Skaggy told him. "As soon as you return with an armed party."

Quiss-an-kweedass raced back to the village. "Kind-a-wuss is alive!" he cried. "She was stolen away by one of the Bear People."

"Bear People!" Women shuddered, for it was something they all feared. "She was stolen away by one of the Bear People?"

The news raced through the village. And when the armed party had gone off, people could talk of little else than the Raven Princess: of what had already happened to her, and of what was still to happen to her. "Surely she's been punished enough," they said. And they noted with relief that the two fathers had once more gone off with the searchers.

"But will they be able to take her away from the Bear People?" they asked one another. And long before it was time, they began to watch impatiently for the return of the armed party.

❧ ❧ ❧

LED BY THE OLD SKAGGY, Quiss-an-kweedass and the fathers and the other armed men were moving on through the vast green wilderness. At long last, they came to a lake.

"That is the lake," the Skaggy said, knowing it from his vision. His piercing eyes searched the shores for a certain large cedar tree.

"Will we be able to take her away from the Bear People?" men muttered to one another, grasping their weapons more firmly.

"We will take her," Quiss-an-kweedass assured them.

The Skaggy moved on around the lake. And the men followed warily. For who knew what Bear People might be watching?

"That is the cedar tree," the Skaggy said, knowing it from his vision. His scrawny finger pointed ahead to where a large cedar tree rose beside the lake.

Moving warily closer to it, they saw a raised house behind it, with a sort of ladder leading up to its door. Standing alone by the lake, the house was carved and painted with unusual Bear totems. It was silent, as if all life had fled from it.

"She is there," the Skaggy told them in his strange, unearthly voice. He turned to Quiss-an-kweedass. "Call her name from the foot of the ladder. And do not be alarmed if she does not know you. For she is under the spell of the Prince of Bears, who loves her as you love her."

The young man's eyes flashed. "I will call her name," he agreed. And when they had reached the cedar tree, he alone went to the foot of the ladder. "Kind-a-wuss!" he called softly.

There was no answer. There was no sound of movement anywhere. Even the birds were silent. Men grasped their weapons.

"Kind-a-wuss!" he called softly, three more times.

On the fourth call, Kind-a-wuss appeared silently at the door. Beautiful as she had always been, but now shrouded with sadness, she looked down at him as if she didn't know him.

"It's I, Quiss-an-kweedass," he said softly. But still she gazed down at him as if she didn't know him.

"I've searched long years for you," he told her. "And now that I've found you, I mean to take you home with me."

"Home?" she murmured. Then her voice suddenly livened. "My children?" she said, glancing about. "They've gone off with their father." And with her mind clearly on her children, she came slowly down the ladder.

The watching fathers and the others rushed in. And though Quiss-an-kweedass only touched her wistfully and waited for her to remember him, her father seized her and carried her off . . . while she cried piteously for her children.

"The Prince of Bears has taken her mind," someone muttered.

❋ ❋ ❋

"SHE'S UNDER A SPELL," people told one another
when the princess was safely back in the village.
And they guarded her tenderly while she still
called for her children.

Then, slowly, she began to know them again.

"Quiss-an-kweedass!" she cried out one day in
glad recognition and rushed into his arms.

Now people really waited to see what would
happen. "Surely she's been punished enough,"
they muttered to one another.

Clearly her parents agreed. The Eagle Prince was
now happily married to the girl he had always
loved. And in any case, Kind-a-wuss, having dishonored her proud title by the terrible thing she
had done, could no longer be married as a princess
should be married. So she was allowed to live with
Quiss-an-kweedass in the house he had built for
her.

"At last they can be happy together," people
said, though they said it with guilty glances.

Yet the two were not truly happy together. A
sadness still shrouded Kind-a-wuss. "My children!
My children!" she cried out from her dreams.

"I'll get your children for you," Quiss-an-
kweedass told her one morning. "Somehow, I'll
take them away from the Prince of Bears."

Her eyes brightened on him. "If you do as I tell
you, my dear, you may not have to *take* them,"
she said. And she taught him the song the Prince
of Bears had often sung to her when he had tried

to make her happy. "Whoever sings the 'Song of the Bears' may have his wish from all bears," he had once confided to her.

It was a sad, wistful song:

I have taken a fair one from her friends as my wife.
I hope her sad friends will not take her away.
I will give her berries from the hills and fish from
*   the streams.*
I will sing her this song and please her always.

🌸 🌸 🌸

THIS TIME, women went with the armed party, because of the children who were to be brought back. The women had learned the plaintive "Song of the Bears." And they sang it softly as they moved through the wilderness toward the lake.

Still singing it, they raised their voices as they moved toward the large cedar tree and the raised house behind it. Standing at the foot of the ladder, they sang:

I have taken a fair one from her friends as my wife.
I hope her sad friends will not take her away.

"Kind-a-wuss!" a voice cried out from the raised house before the song could be finished. And as a handsome young man, the Prince of Bears rushed down the ladder to greet his lost love, with two small boys scrambling down behind him.

But Kind-a-wuss was not there.

"Prince of Bears, she is sad because of her children," Quiss-an-kweedass said, glancing at the two small boys clinging to their father. "She wishes you to send her children to her."

"No!" the Prince of Bears cried out, holding his sons close.

Men tightened their grasp on their weapons. But the wiser women began to sing:

I have taken a fair one from her friends as my wife.
I hope her sad friends will not take her away.
I will give her berries from the hills and fish from
the streams.
I will sing her this song and please her always.

"I will please her always," the Prince of Bears said, thrusting his sons from him. Then, almost blinded by his tears, he rushed back up the ladder.

❦ ❦ ❦

"My children! My children!" Kind-a-wuss cried out when they reached the village. She folded the confused children to her, holding them close until they, in turn, began to cling to her.

"Now she will be happy," people told one another.

She would have been very happy had it not been for one small son. This son pined for his father, for the raised house by the lake, and for the bears he had played with.

One day, listening as he often did at the edge of

the forest, he said, "My father has come to take me home." And without another word, he ran off into the forest.

Kind-a-wuss laid a quick hand on Quiss-an-kweedass's arm to stop him from going after the boy. "We must let him do what he must do," she said, blinking back tears. "And it will make his father happy." Then she sang the "Song of the Bears" to her other small son.

The song was her great gift to the clan she had dishonored. And so great was the gift that it lifted all further shame from her name, forever. For it was as the Prince of Bears had said, "Whoever sings the 'Song of the Bears' may have his wish from all bears."

To this day, there are children who sing the "Song of the Bears" on the big offshore islands of the Haida. And perhaps they do get their wish from the bears.

Story Sources

A. THE INDIAN LEGENDS:

During the past two centuries, the rich native cultures of our Northwest Coast have almost vanished into the more dominant immigrant cultures. But, fortunately for us, there have always been concerned people to record the songs and stories before they were forgotten. And although variants of the tales have been found, the basic sources for those in this book were:

1899 *Tales from the Totems of the Hidery* recorded by James Deans for the Archives of the International Folk-Lore Association.

1905 *Kwakiutl Texts.* Vol. III, recorded by Franz Boas and George Hunt for The Jesup North Pacific Expedition, Memoir of the American Museum of Natural History.

1907 *Folktales and Myths* recorded by C. Hill-Tout for a chapter of his book, *British North America, The Far West,* in the series, The Native Races of the British Empire.

1909   *Tlingit Myths and Texts* recorded by John R. Swanton for the Smithsonian Institution, Bureau of American Ethnology, Bulletin 39.

1953   *Haida Myths Illustrated in Argillite Carvings* recorded by Marius Barbeau for the National Museum of Canada, Bulletin No. 127, Anthropolical Series No. 32.

B.   FAIRY TALES FOR THE PREAMBLES:

The fairy tales referred to can be found in the *Blue, Red, Green, Crimson, Orange, Rose, Yellow, Violet, Olive, Grey, Olive* or *Brown Fairy Books*, collected and edited by Andrew Lang, or in *Dragons, Dragons, Dragons,* edited by Helen Hoke, or in *The Fairy Ring* of tales collected by Kate Douglas Wiggin.